for John and Patty Fitts

A Special Thanks to Susan Wolf Johnson, Cameron MacKenzie, Reginald McKnight, Stephanie Allen, Laura Strachan, Panio Gianopolis, Kelly Falconer, Kathleen Volk Miller, Marc Vincenz, Linda Gallant and Nathaniel Popkin.

A Very Special Thanks to John Beck, Todd Stark, Jeff Smith, Eric Beard, Jeff Mosely, Adam Kilgore, Suzy Beers, Tracy Real, Jessica Beck and Chuck Purvis.

Table of Contents

*Your troubles are the reward of years
of climbing invisible hills....*
—Mitch Easter

No Rabia

Chloe asked Lee if the mercurochrome would sting, and Lee said that it wouldn't. She asked if she even needed to use it, and he told her that if she had read *The Snows of Kilimanjaro*, she would know.

"Do you think it's rabid?"

"I don't know. Rabid dogs attack, and that dog attacked," Lee said.

"Do you think I can get AIDS?"

"Can you get AIDS from a dog? I don't think so," he said. "I don't think AIDS can jump species. Or it can, maybe."

She asked him if wasn't that the way humans got HIV in the first place, and he said she was right, but that it had been primate—primate, not canine—primate, but she could sure as hell catch rabies.

Chloe had stopped crying, but she was still shaking. The bite had two puncture wounds, and the surrounding skin had already begun to take on shades of purple. She asked what would happen if the dog was rabid, and he told her that she didn't need to worry about it, because the bellboy would be there any second, and they were going to find the fucking dog, and if it was rabid, she would have to get some shots. "Don't worry. Rabies is like tetanus. You can get a shot after you are exposed."

"How long after?"

"I don't know. Not too goddamned much later." Lee opened the bottle of Herradura and poured a half-inch into the glass by the night stand. "You don't want to dilly-dally. I mean, if you

1

think you have rabies, then you want to get on the stick."

"What if I don't get the shots?" she asked him, and he told her that she would go insane, and not a pretty insanity, but a nervous sort of maelstrom, and she would die. She started crying again, and there was a knock at the door.

"It's him," Lee said. "He'll have good news."

"How do you know?"

"Hunch." Lee threw a flannel over his t-shirt and opened the door. "*Hola*," Lee said to the bellboy, who stood at the entrance.

"*Hola*, hello." The bellboy stood no taller than five-five, his hair combed across the top of his head in the fashion of a bad toupee, but he was clearly no older than twenty-eight. He smiled and bounced on his heels as they talked, as if they were all three about to head off for a night on the strip.

"Did you find the owner?" Lee asked.

"Good news," the bellboy seemed as relieved as they Lee and Chloe. "The owner said it is okay. The dog is healthy. She can show you the papers tomorrow and give you proof."

Lee said to the bellboy, then turned sideways to include Chloe in the conversation to avoid repeating himself, "The dog needs to be tested. They have to test the dog."

"*Sí, sí*. It does not need the test. It is *no rabioso*."

"Christ," Lee said. "You think I should call the cops on her? I mean, what the fuck was the dog doing running around out there?"

"Um," the bellboy paused. "It is not the dog's fault, you see. She explained this. It is the *guard* dog, but the dog cannot go outside during the day, because of the people. The dog does not have much chance to go to the bathroom and run. So, as you can imagine, it is excited when it goes out. You know?"

"What about a fence?"

"Fence?"

"Jesus God."

Chloe brought each of them a glass of the sugarcane liquor on ice. The bellboy thanked her, and the two drank it in one shot, winced and shook it off.

"So you went there at the wrong time," the bellboy said.

"What?"

"You should not go there when the dog is going outside."

"How do I know when the dog goes outside?"

The bellboy looked at his watch and said, "About an hour ago."

"How was I supposed to know?"

"It goes out every night. Same time."

"I'm gonna call the cops tomorrow morning," Lee said.

"Oh, not necessary."

"Why not?"

"The dog is safe. *No rabioso.*"

"But it bites."

"Of course. It is a *guard* dog."

"But there are people out there," Lee said.

"Not many," he said, chuckling. "Actually, there are usually never people out there at night. It is not safe. They have a guard dog."

The strategy was brilliant, Lee mused. What better way to deter criminals than letting the guard dog *out*, though he kept this observation to himself. "I'm calling the cops," Lee held the glass to his lips as if to take a sip, then tipped the glass toward the bellboy and said, "You want more?"

"Okay. *Gracias.* One more. It is strong, right?" he said, then smiled.

"It is strong," Lee said and poured the bellboy another shot.

"It is none of my business," the bellboy said, "but why were you on the street?"

"We were coming back from a restaurant."

"Walking?"

"We took the subway. We walked home from the Zocalo subway station."

"*Subway*? Why? You take the Sitio. It is *night*."

"Subways are only fifteen cents," Lee said.

"You are from *Estados Unidos*. You have money."

* * *

Each of the first ten nights in Mexico it had rained. The mornings started off beautiful, crisp, foreshadowings of autumn in the July air, then the afternoons turned brutal, choking with pollution and heat. Torrents rolled in an hour before sundown, and the evening alternated between drizzle, fog and more torrents. They tried to escape the rain and took a bus up to Taxco, but at night a fine mist, evidently, had been creeping up the mountainside with such regularity that the streets had developed a thin green moss, which turned slick at the very mention of moisture, making any attempt at traversing the roads after dark a feat worthy of prime-time reality TV. After two nights, they returned to Mexico City.

Lee and Chloe had decided to go to Mexico City when the director of Lee's first play told him to get lost. Lee was making surprise visits to rehearsal, then sitting in the shadows and objecting to phrasings, hand gestures, and even demanding that the lead actor be fired. With just three weeks left until opening night, the director spoke frankly to Lee. "I love this play, but I do not like you. Get lost." Chloe told Lee to stick around anyway—screw that hotshot grad student and his patchouli. It's *your* play. Your play. Lee had considered this, but it had become tedious, and he was increasingly worried about what his friends and family would think about the play. "It's his play now," Lee said. "I can't stop it at this point," and they booked a trip to Mexico to prevent him from changing his mind and barging down to the theatre.

Lee had hoped to use the three weeks away to forget about the play and try to get an objective handle on the whole thing. They would go down south, stock their room with tequila, get a bunch of cigars and reset the machine, but Chloe continued her campaign to go after the director. "Grow a pair and can his ass," she had said on the bus to Taxco, on the hairpin mountain roads, moments after Lee had been certain that the bus had run over a farmer and his two baby donkeys.

"Who's going to direct it?"

"*You.*"

"Where was this advice before the trip?"

"I'm just saying."

On the way back to Mexico City she badgered him about the decision to use a male nurse. "A male nurse," she said. "Why a *male* nurse?"

"Jesus Christ," Lee said.

"Is there a specific reason?"

"Does there need to be?"

"If it can be played by a woman, sure. A role traditionally played by women, is suddenly played by a man? For no reason? If there isn't any reason, then it's a little weird, don't you think?"

"Maybe he performed well on the casting couch. Can we drop it?" he said.

When they had escaped the rain into a café to wait out the weather over *cervesas* and *sopés* and a couple shots, Chloe asked the waiter if it always rained like this in Mexico. The waiter said that sometimes it does not rain at all, but sometimes it rains much more. He began to walk away, then stopped and said that sometimes it rains just about like this. Lee told Chloe that it was getting to the point where every time he took off his socks he was beginning to crave wine and cheese. "There is more fungus on my feet than feet."

"That's disgusting."

"It is disgusting," he said then lit a cigarette.

Lee ordered a beer and another plate of *sopés*. He lit a cigarette. It was still raining outside, and two mariachi players appeared at the entrance. They were obviously musicians that played for tourists, not the real deal. The two musicians could barely stand, and when they began to play, Lee and Chloe could tell they were playing mariachi music only because they were wearing mariachi outfits, and because the larger player, an obese man with hands like hams, shouted, "Mariachi! When the food and drinks arrived, Chloe took a cigarette from Lee's pack of Delicados, sipped from her tequila, moved the shot of tomato juice to the side and said, "So what did your folks say about the play?"

"They said, 'You wrote a play?'"

"Funny."

"They did," he said.

"They didn't know you were writing a play about them?"

"It's not about them. It's a play."

"They didn't even know you were writing a play?"

"I can't tell them everything."

"You're a playwright. Shouldn't they expect you to be writing plays?"

"Then, see? I don't have to tell them."

"Well, I've been on the edge of my seat."

"About their opinion of the play?"

"Yes, you know," she said, dragging the cigarette. "This is your grand renunciation. Isn't it going to cause some drama?"

"What renunciation?"

"Of Christ. This is it."

"Whoa, sister. The play isn't my big renunciation of Christ. Nobody is renouncing anything. The characters are renouncing Christ, kind of—some characters, but some don't. If you've read it, which you obviously have, then you would know that some of the characters have their faith *affirmed*."

"No, they don't. The protagonist feels a stir, but it is clear that it is the image of the Christ Child that creates the stir, the manifestation of the Christ Child that he intends to *sell*."

"The protagonist. The primary character."

"He is pressured into selling the root. The protagonist feels a stir. The stir is the issue. No stir, no play."

"You may have written it that way, but I didn't read it that way."

"Sorry, babe, it's my play."

"Sorry, Mister, not anymore. It belongs to me now, and anyone else who sees it or reads it. It is clear that you have renounced Christ. I don't understand how anyone can write a play like that and still believe in that stuff. It's certainly a commentary."

Lee had had a string of one-act plays that had been performed in festivals in the Northeast, all of which had been successful, in terms of audience appreciation, reviews and invitations to have more plays performed. In his first full-length production, the protagonist discovers an Asian root that has dried and warped until it becomes a near identical image of the Christ Child. The root captures the attention of his family, who are equally interested in the bids that the protagonist has received for said root, which had already surpassed the dollar amounts of the pretzel, and even the grilled-cheese Mary.

"Don't tell me you believe that crap," Chloe said. "You don't, do you?"

"How long have we been together? My position has always been very clear."

7

"That you don't believe that crap."

"I never said that I do or do not believe anything. My position is that I feel, as a result of my early indoctrination, that I am simply incapable of having faith. Would I like to have faith? Sure, who wouldn't? But for me, faith has been replaced by OCD and fear," Lee said, turning his attention to the mariachi players. "If those assholes don't stop playing in five minutes, I'm going to say something."

"But you would rather believe in Jesus than Buddha."

"I would rather not be the one who determines that there is any real difference."

"Then you will renounce Christ for me?" she said, taking a Delicado from the pack.

"For you."

"Of course. Is it wrong for me to ask you?" she said, shooting the tomato juice, then sipping the tequila. "Listen, people convert for each other all the time. Is this any different? I'm just asking you to do the opposite."

"Good God. I'm not going to *renounce* anything. One day I feel one way, the next day I feel another. I'm not going to renounce *anything*."

"So you think I'm going to hell."

"I'm not sure if hell even exists. Did you know that Jesus never even mentioned the word *hell*?"

"But you think I'm going to hell."

"My hope is that there is no hell. I have never really been able to figure out the function of a real hell. What is the function of hell? The great thing about all major religions is that they get people to help and forgive each other. They keep order. What could be the function of hell?"

"Are you asking me?" she said. "There is no hell. It doesn't serve any function."

"I'm asking you to speculate. To step out of your unbelievably liberated self and participate in a discussion of possible functions of hell," Lee waited a moment while Chloe lit a cigarette, then sipped his beer and said, "That has always been my great hope. That there is no real hell, that there are no stakes. Just a matter of faith. You believe, fine. You don't, fine. Ever since I was four years old, it has always been my great hope that neither hell nor heaven existed, but that we could just go somewhere medium, that we could understand who is right or wrong and then come to some sort of reconciliation with the whole scheme of things."

"I can't believe I'm dating a Christian."

Lee and Chloe ordered espresso, shot it down, settled up and left.

"Let's grab a Sitio," Lee said to Chloe.

"I'm taking the subway."

"It's ten-thirty," Lee said. Outside, the raining had stopped. The streets shone, and the air felt clean in their lungs. They were surprised that it was only ten-thirty. The flashing neon bars seemed to have jumped out of nowhere.

* * *

How could he believe that crap? He had never given any clues that he was religious. Chloe occasionally walked downstairs on Sunday mornings to find him sitting Indian style with a bowl of cereal and mug of coffee watching shows directly from the Crystal Cathedral. These sermons horrified him more than any scary movie. The hypnotic lull to the rhetoric, the foggy glaze over the minister's voice, the oppressive, redundant sermons, the same points being made over and over, the total lack of humor, the laughter on cue, the call for tithes, the infusion of the most unforgiving politics, and the right of the wealthy to enjoy God's blessings. He wondered why, if God existed, then why He would

9

allow these churches to exist. Would He send some kind of fireball down to incinerate these churches? Or less extreme, wouldn't he just clog up the logistics that made them possible? Wouldn't God just inspire handfuls of people to form little spiritual cells all over the country that might offer more viability to their beliefs?

* * *

The scene on the way back to the hotel from the restaurant had reminded Lee of middle-school hero/love kung fu fantasies: empty street, gates, corrugated metal pulled down over shop entrances, broken windows on second story apartments, black sky and rats—everything dirty-brownish under the yellow street lights, like sepia-toned photographs from the nineteen-fifties. In his middle-school fantasies, though, the girl at his side was not Chloe, but Alison Chambers, his twelve-year-old trampoline buddy and number-one crush—the kind of girl whom he daydreamed about defending. In these fantasies, not only did Lee defeat bullies and jocks to defend her honor, but figures emerged from the shadows, one by one, two by two, three by three and as many as he could imagine, and he would knock them over like bowling pins with roundhouse kicks and homemade nunchucks with moves that would make Jackie Chan wet his shorts. But when he and Chloe realized that they must have taken the wrong turn out of the subway and ended up in the alleyways behind the Zocalo instead of the entrance to the Hotel Canada, he did not welcome the catcalls from the shadows. The two travelers pretended not to hear, picked up their pace in such a subtle fashion that only those who preyed upon travelers and the weak would notice. A tighter grip on his arm and a stiffening of his legs signaled that they were not, in fact, armed, but ready to absorb blows before getting stuffed into a trunk, slashed up with a two-dollar switchblade, or a finger snipped off before being driven around from ATM to ATM to max out credit cards. They were suckers, and they knew it, but for one reason or the next, they made it. At the corner of the next street, they saw the street vendor who sold them Bohemia Cervezas and bottled water, who sat in front of the cafe where they bought tacos.

Both Lee and Chloe sighed upon seeing the beer seller. They had walked through the Valley of the Shadow of Death, feared evil, and passed through unharmed. God had had mercy on them despite their fear and stupidity, and they relaxed. Then they noticed the beer seller look across the street. Something was about to happen. They had relaxed too soon, Lee knew. Did the beer seller see figures emerging from the shadows, or flints of metal flicker in the streetlamps? They turned to see what the man was looking at, and a dog, knee-high, dirty white and baring fangs, charged at Lee, who suddenly froze while the dog shifted and scooted around Chloe's legs, taking a nip at her calf. Instinctively, Lee kicked the dog in the ribs. The dog, turned his attention to Lee and tore into his sneakers, but he had lucked out. The teeth had missed his toes.

His semi-heroics did not go unnoticed, however. When he washed her wound and took out the bottle of mercurochrome, she said, "You love me, don't you." He said that of course he loved her. Of course he *loved* her.

* * *

The morning bellboy, with some hesitation, took Lee to the site of the incident from the evening before. His hangover was something from ancient prophecies. What was he thinking with that sugarcane stuff? Some kind of distilled go-cart fuel. The alley from which the dog had darted was packed with a Konica camera shop, jewelry shop and a cobbler. The end of the alley opened up to a wide-open area, a combination between a garage and courtyard, surrounded by wrought iron railings and apartments.

A Coca-Cola can on a workbench in the back seemed to be set off by the black and white surroundings—puddles of oil on the concrete floor, the iron railings and staircase in the corner, the once-white walls streaked with grease and mildew, and two incandescent light bulbs hanging by single wires washing away any colors besides the can of cola. Had the picture been in a movie, the Coca-Cola can would have stood out as implausibly overt product placement. But the scene was not black and white. Off center stood a bright yellow shack with a single open window. Above the window read a sign in blue paint, "Dentist Dave." The entire morning was a mistake, he knew. The hangover itself bordered on medical emergency. He wondered if she would have done the same for him.

The two clerks nodded at him, then at each other.

Lee asked for a sheet of paper and a ballpoint pen, and after some confusion, the clerk slid his request across the glass-top counter. "Thank you," Lee said. "*Gracias*," and proceeded to draw a picture of a dog with two spots on his back and gigantic fangs biting a young woman.

"Last night?" one man said.

"Yes," Lee said.

"The dog?"

"Yes."

"The man from the hotel?"

"Yes," Lee said. "He came here about the dog."

"*Si! Si!*" the two men behind the counter said, as if they suddenly understood the conversation. "Coco!"

"Coco?"

"No worry," the man said, "*No rabioso.*" The next man nodded his head in agreement, driving the point home, "*no rabioso.*"

Lee lit a cigarette, inhaled, and said, "Yes, but how do I know?"

"Because it is *no rabioso*. If it has *no rabia*, it cannot be *rabioso*."

The next man broke in and tried to clarify the issue, "First there must be *rabia*. If there is *rabia*, then the dog can be *rabioso*, *si?* But here, there is *no rabia*, so the dog is *no rabioso*."

"In Mexico? There is *no rabia* in Mexico?"

"Of course, there is *rabia* in Mexico. There is much *rabia* in Mexico!"

The next man agreed, "It is a serious problem, *rabia*. Mexico has terrible *rabia*."

"Many dogs are *rabioso* in Mexico."

"That is why Coco is *no rabioso*. Coco is the guard dog. To have a guard dog *rabioso* is crazy."

A young woman entered through the back door, along with an old woman. The young woman looked at one of the men and laughed. "She talked to the man, no?"

"Yes."

"And she told you, no?"

"Told me what?"

"She told you it is okay. *No rabioso*."

Lee wanted to explain the nature of his hangover, and that he was in no mood, but instead, he pressed his palm into his forehead.

An old woman, with her scalp visible beneath a bad perm, clutching her arms to her breasts, entered through the alley and walked behind the counter. The woman's face seemed to be stuck in permanent fright, as if she had been abused so long that her eyebrows became fixed in a furrow, and her lips naturally pulled away from her teeth as if her skull were slowly emerging from her face. Coco tried to jump from the woman's arms, as if Lee were someone to play with, or at least check out.

Coco: a testament to man's silly notion towards sentimentality.

To have this ragged little beast climbing on one's bed, licking your face, walking on your carpet, probably drinking out of the toilet and begging for food on a constant basis, and undoubtedly stinking like a shitstorm—to have this animal roaming one's house seemed unthinkable, but Coco was clearly crazy about the frightened old woman. Rabid dogs bite, but they don't cozy. Lee assumed the woman's face seemed stuck in permanent fright because she was permanently frightened. That's what happens. Nice old ladies have nice old faces. Old playboys look rugged. Mean old people have mean old faces, and scared people look scared.

The bellboy told Lee that the man in the garage can show him the papers. "He has the paper," the bellboy said. "He can show you."

"Dentist Dave?"

"He's the one," the bellboy said.

They knocked on the shack and the door opened. Sure enough, the sign was true. On the walls hung an assortment of dentistry tools of varying sterility, tubes attached to tanks, and in the center of the shack, a modified barber's chair with a man, arms to the side, legs slightly apart, and an arrangement of rubber bands and hooks holding the man's mouth open. The man whom Lee surmised to be Dentist Dave surprised him the most. He stood several inches taller than everyone, bald, with a curly black waxed mustache, as if he belonged to some nineteen thirties circus troupe and had gotten mixed up with time machines, then decided to while away his days posing as a dentist in Mexico City. Dentist Dave looked at the bellboy and nodded to Lee, then to the old woman. He held up a sheet of paper and said, "*No rabisoo.*"

* * *

As it happened, the play turned out to be his big renunciation after all. His parents flew up to DC for opening night, despite his protestations. They would have none of it. "Nothing we did in this lifetime deserves a child like this," his father had said over the phone and e-mailed him the flight information. As a surprise, his brother's family also showed up for the event.

Lee explained that if you don't get paid anything for a production, technically it isn't any big deal, so his father cut him a check. "Now it's a big deal. Can you please shut up and let us enjoy the play?"

After the performance, they went to an Italian restaurant in Adam's Morgan, where he ordered a branzino, and his parents chose the veal, which came with much too much red sauce for his mother's biliary gland. Chloe ordered a vodka, and his brother's family left early for the hotel. They needed to get to the airport early, and their appetites weren't what they should be. They were bushed. Aside from the brief conversations regarding gall bladders and glands, the conversation at the restaurant ran fairly quiet on the family scale. When the fish arrived, his mother made the waiter return it because the eyeballs were still in the fish's head. Chloe informed them that in China, you can order fish where only the body is dipped in hot oil, and the head is actually still alive while you eat it.

"Thanks for the details, babe," Lee said, "now I can throw up right here at the table."

He ordered a vodka for himself, and after a few moments of silence, his mother broke the tension. "I just wish, for a minute, for one minute, you could know what it is like to carry a baby in your own body for nine months, to have the baby's body actually be part of your own body, then find out that the baby will be going to hell. That's what I wish."

"Is that a toast?" Lee said. "Are we toasting to my success?"

Chloe hit the table. "That's exactly what the mother said in the play. *Line* for *line*. Word for word. That is unbelievable."

"It's a request," his mother said to Lee. "If you could feel that sensation for one minute, then you wouldn't write about the things you write about. You could write about good things."

"I wish I didn't write about anything."

"You can write about anything you want to. That's your choice. But if you knew what it was like to have one of your children going to hell, you wouldn't write about things like that. You would write about interesting things—why do people feel like they have to be depressing to be creative?"

"I need a cigarette. I'm gonna cut my ball off if I don't have a cigarette."

"And you smoke. Your grandfathers, both of them had their lungs cut in half, and you still smoke. Cut in half."

It was true. Both of his grandfathers had almost exactly half of each lung carved out of their chests, living their remaining years wheezing and coughing their brains out.

"Think about that," his mother said. "Think about the oxygen tanks."

"The protagonist feels a stir. The protagonist discovers the root and feels a stir. That's the thing. What do you think the stir is?"

"Demons."

"This is *unbelievable*," Chloe said. "This is note for note."

"Jesus, Mary and hellfire," Lee said.

"He's a good person," Chloe cut in. "Lee tries not to be a good person, but he is. He's a good person. He tries to be bad, but he isn't. He tries to drink a lot, but he gets sleepy. He's never cheated on me. I have friends who have put the moves on him— *good* friends—and he almost has, but he breaks down and can't do it. Do you know how long we were together before he would even sleep with me?"

"They're my fucking parents," Lee said, scanning the horizon for the waiter.

"This is all age-appropriate," she said. "You think they want you to be lonely your entire life?"

"Yes, they *do*." Lee took out a cigarette and lit up. Chloe told him that they weren't in the smoking section, but he told her to chill for a second.

"He is good," she reiterated. "He saved my life while we were in Mexico."

"I didn't save anybody's life."

"You should tell us things," his mother said. "You're ashamed of being a hero and a writer. I just don't know why you can't write plays that don't denigrate Christ."

"I write one play about a man who struggles with his religious identity and the Pharisees that swim around him like sharks. Nothing in the play denigrates Christ."

"The nurse said the root looked like a turd," Chloe said.

"That was his own *flawed* interpretation of Christ."

"I didn't get that," his father said.

"He actually did save my life," Chloe said. She scooted her chair back and showed them two purple scars where the teeth marks had just about skinned over.

"Had the dog been rabid, I would have saved her life, but the dog was not rabid, so there was no life to save; there was only the confirmation of health."

"It was probably a coyote," the mother said. "I can't believe it didn't kill you."

"It was a dog," Lee said. "Coco. Coco nipped her."

"It probably did have rabies," his mother said.

"Rabid dogs attack," his father said. "You have to kill those dogs."

"I didn't kill it," Lee said.

"You didn't kill it, but you had it killed," Chloe said.

"I had it examined after it was put to sleep," Lee said.

"That's right," his father said, then explained, in full detail, the only way to test for rabies. "You have to take the brain out. You freeze it, slice the cerebral cortex, then test each slice for inflammation. If you don't get the dog, then there's no telling if there is any inflammation. Don't worry about those animal lovers when it comes to things like rabies. Just cut their heads off and do the test."

"So there was no inflammation," his mother said. "There was no inflammation, right?"

"Tell him the story," Chloe said. "This is why I like dating a playwright. They walk around everywhere with a prepared mind."

"One man's prepared mind is another man's Asperger's," Lee said, then after a moment of uncomfortable silence, he told them the story. He said that there wasn't anything really fascinating about it at all. He recalled the holocaust of brain cells from the sugar cane liquor he drank with the bellboys, the hangover that made the pull of gravity on his teeth actually hurt.

"Stretching cures hangovers," his father said. "Stretch it out."

"Sex cures hangovers," Chloe said.

"Nobody stop her," Lee said.

"Factually, it does," Chloe said, "but it only cures hangovers while you're having sex. Once you stop the hangover returns. So you have to—well," she said. "You just have to keep doing it."

Lee embarked on the story he had tried out during the plane trip back to DC on an older couple they sat next to. They also had had enough of the rain, and the husband told them that all the Imodium in the world couldn't keep him away from a bathroom. The couple on the plane loved the bellboy, and the husband told Lee that he had even used the same type of wire loop device to rescue a dog during the war that Lee and the police had used to catch Coco.

The second vodka finally arrived. He tells them how the cop was able to apprehend Coco with little trouble, and how the dog instantly curled up into a little ball of fury, and the bellboy stuck the dog in the ass, and you could see the stuff working all the way up. "The leg goes limp, then the tail uncurls, the front paws relax, the fangs sink back into the snout, then the lights go out and that's a wrap. It would have been a wrap, but as they're stuffing Coco into a canvas bag, the old lady sinks down behind the counter like they're taking her son to the gallows. Some of the clerks are comforting her, and the girl freaks out and starts swiping at the air and flashing her nails like a fistful of razors. It was terrifying, and before you know it, the old woman wakes up and starts heaving haymakers. It's like a cross between and a bad Mexican soap opera and a prison riot. The cop has his nightstick out, cocking it back and pumping out little half-swings, but he can't figure out who to hit, the glass countertop breaks, and it all stops on a dime when the bellboy, this guy, with his hair tumbling on his head like a toupee, and the whole thing is so surreal, that he would not have believed it had he not been there, but this bellboy—as if his feet levitated off the ground, and even though everyone is going at it pretty viciously, and had anyone said this guy would have been capable of that kind of violence before that morning, he would have never believed them, but that bellboy, in the middle of a cartoonish swirl of fists and hair and dust and spit and broken glass, this bellboy elevates and coldcocks the old lady—just drops her like a sack of beets. The bellboy raises, pulls his fist back and pops her right under the eye, and you can hear that one individual smack, meat on meat, above all the mayhem. It divides the chaos like a chemical reaction. Oil pulls away from water and they keep separating, back out of the door, and somewhere on the way to the clinic, the bellboy makes himself scarce, and suddenly it's just me and the cop. We even stop for *sopés* and a glass of *cervesa* and coffee, and he lets me pick up the tab. And the doctor even lets me sit in on the procedure to test for rabies."

"Don't tell. Do not tell me the procedure," his mother said. "Don't tell me anything. Let's go back to the way we were."

"And it was official. *No rabisoo*."

"That is the greater good," his father said. "The woman doesn't get hit, that fight keeps going, and from the sounds of it, you were outnumbered. We're lucky we didn't have to go down to Mexico to get you out of jail or pick up your remains. You don't screw around with rabies."

"And I didn't," Lee said. He eyeballed the waiter and motioned for another.

* * *

Chloe's antics provided the exact opposite reaction that he had anticipated. She even talked his parents into a couple vodkas and she told them the entire story all over again, about the really cool guy they met in Taxco, who was totally out of the loop, and how they had almost been killed when their bus had nearly lost control on the mountainside.

The play would run its course, its pathetic ten performances, which didn't seem at all pathetic six months prior. The sounds from the restaurant blurred together with the sound of his parents and Chloe, yammering away, all with a full head of gusto. Lee's father wanted to know more about that hangover cure, and his mother deadpanned, saying that it sounded like a whole lot of fun. Lee let his mind glaze over, and for a moment he looked for the clearest route to the exit, but then he settled in. A thought occurred to him. If there was a venue for a short full-length play, he would write it. Somewhere between a one-act and a full-length. Five characters in a garage, five blocks from the Zocalo. One dentist, one tourist, one patient, one bellboy, one frightened old lady, one dog. The dentist explains that when one pulls a tooth, technique is of the utmost importance. It is very easy, in fact. He explains how they tested the theory on cadavers in dental school. You can pull straight out with all your might, all day long, and that tooth isn't going to budge. You will do neck damage before you do tooth damage. *Your* neck. But with a simple flick of the wrist, just like that, the tooth pops out. Even a child can do it. "Now. You try," Dentist Dave says to the tourist. "Do you believe me?" The tourist says that he does believe him, one hundred percent.

"Then try," the dentist says to the tourist. The old woman looks more frightened, and the bellboy clucks his tongue against the roof of his mouth. The dentist helps the tourist on to the chair, where he awkwardly straddles the patient. "Like this?" he says, flipping his wrist in the air. The dentist laughs and tells him no, to pull out. Pull out hard, any tooth, and the tourist obeys. He has to lean forward and pull the man's head towards him, and his positioning proves too awkward to do anything, but then he gets his angle and a good grip. At first he is unsure that he will keep his balance, but he does. He gains a good ergonomic position that allows him to use his legs, dig in, and he leans back and pulls with all his might.

Does Anything Beautiful Emerge?

Jackson was intent on catching a bullfrog. He said it was easy. All you had to do was estimate the direction of the frog's leap and time it to the exact moment of the frog's reaction. Then you had it. You have to sneak up on it, but once you do that, all you had to do was predict the time and direction.

"No shit," Fisher said.

"You got a better plan?"

"Yeah, a net."

The three boys had gotten sidetracked at the pond while walking to the school. They had decided on the location after Marlon told them that the janitors always left the side door open on the far end of the church. He and his neighbor had gone in last week. They had taken the shortcut by the soccer field and walked up Old Tyler Road. They had made their way into the girl's locker room, rifled through the desks of all the teachers, and even found a chamber above the pulpit where you could observe the congregation on Sunday mornings without anybody knowing. Once you got into the church, all you had to do was wander through the halls to the back, and the door connecting to the school didn't even have a lock. It was that easy, Marlon told them, and they headed off. But after they trekked down Savoy from Jackson's house, they turned up on South Saunders Road and heard a water sound where the drain from the pond emptied into a ditch. "Shit," Jackson said. "Those are bullfrogs," and jumped down to have a closer inspection.

Jackson said if they could get one bullfrog, they could cut

it up, tie the pieces to milk jugs, and catch a bunch of snapping turtles. They could all sneak out at night and meet up. They could jump the fence and put the jugs out into the water. Come back in the morning and get the turtles.

"What are we going to do with snapping turtles?" Fisher asked.

"Sell 'em," Jackson said. "Plenty of people would buy snapping turtles. Everybody wants a snapping turtle."

Marlon said nobody's going to catch a bullfrog with their bare hands, and nobody's going to catch a snapping turtle. You could try your whole life and you wouldn't be able to do it. If you wanted a bullfrog, you had to come out at night with a gig and a flashlight, and then you look for beady red eyes, and the light beam paralyzes them. That's when you stick them. But you have to have your bucket and your jugs all ready. You don't do one thing on one day then the other thing another day. Plus, you don't do any of it unless you have a *market*. If you know somebody who wants a snapping turtle, then you do it. You do it if the price they are willing to pay is worth the time and effort and your expenses. "You don't go to all the trouble with the vague hope that you *might* find somebody willing to buy a snapping turtle. Sure, people out there want to buy snapping turtles, but do you know them personally?"

"I'll figure out who," Jackson said.

"Besides," Marlon said, "we come here at night, walk around with flashlights, somebody's liable to start shooting at us with rock salt."

"Marlon's a pussy," Jackson said.

"You two are small time," Marlon said. "Bullfrogs. Snapping turtles."

"Forget about the bullfrogs," Fisher said, suggesting they keep on walking to the school. They should go inside and turn everything upside down. "We should steal all the chalk and erasers."

"Smash all the mirrors in the bathroom," Jackson said.

They thought about other types of mayhem. They mused upon going into the walk-in refrigerator, dumping milk on all of the carpets and making the entire building stink, turning over the library shelves, changing all of the grades or stealing the gradebooks altogether, bending the legs of the chairs so they all wobbled. Fisher said they should steal some toilet paper from the janitor's closet and roll some houses. Buy a couple dozen eggs at the grocery store.

"Again, small time," Marlon said.

"Again, Marlon's a pussy," Jackson said.

Marlon said he wasn't a pussy, it's just that all of their ideas ended up making their own lives more difficult. Stinking up their own classrooms rooms with rancid milk, sitting in uneven chairs, making pissed off teachers re-grade them. Marlon said if he was going to do something at all, he was going to do it big. He wasn't going to trash any classrooms, break any mirrors or anything like that. If he was going to do anything, he was going to go big. All that stuff was petty vandalism. If he was going to fuck with them, he was going to fuck with them. You could burn the whole school down in an hour. "Less than an hour," Marlon said. "Guaranteed. All you have to do is pull the fire alarm, get everybody out, and burn the place down. I can get some sodium from my dad's lab. We could pack the sodium in a shell of sugar and flush a couple cubes down the toilet. By the time the sugar melts, all hell breaks loose. Or we could sneak in some gasoline, hide it in the janitor's closet on Friday, show up Saturday morning, climb up into the ceiling tiles and pour it down the inside of the walls. We do it on all four corners of the school. Keep the windows shut so the fumes build up. Flush the sodium, leave a trail of rubbing alcohol to the hallway. You could make the place one big bomb. Turn the place into an actual inferno." Marlon then presented the other two with an image. The school itself, three stories high, one hundred fifty feet in length, burning from all sides, flames catching wind and forming a vortex. He told them that it is entirely possible during forest fires for the wind to create small tornados consisting solely of flame. "Imagine that," Marlon said. "Our school, a monolith of fire licking the sky. It would be like the Earth opening up and swallowing that shithole," Marlon said. "If we do anything at all, we do something big, like that."

Just two years prior, the boys had practiced school spirit with nationalistic fervor. They wore their Shades Mountain Bible soccer uniforms all day after games, green Adidas jerseys with white shorts with the built-in jock and the three stripes down the side. The varsity team had won the State finals two consecutive years, and students at Shades Mountain Bible Academy walked with pride. In the autumn and winter they donned nylon green jackets with an Eagle patch sewn to the back and chevrons stitched to the sleeves signifying years of athletic service.

But then things took a turn. Newschannel 6 showed up one weekday morning at Shades Mountain Bible after Pastor Vincent had delivered a mandate that each student bring to school an item that causes him or her to stumble in their Walk with the Lord. And by stumble, Pastor Vincent explained that it could be anything—not just dirty magazines, chewing tobacco, televisions, or rock albums, but anything that distracted you from your quiet time, your tithing, your prayer life, your anything. It could be a bicycle, favorite shirt, favorite socks, favorite cereal. If you awoke in the morning thinking about cereal before Jesus, bring in the cereal.

In a single day, the school's fortune shifted. Newschannel 6 created a montage of images—students standing behind shimmering heat waves and smoke, teachers tossing baseball gloves and money onto the pile of char, a shot of Pastor Vincent observing his handiwork, standing stoic behind a sheet of white smoke. The exodus of normal students concentrated the children of fanatics, and those left behind could feel their skin bluing in the Appalachian foothills, the sounds of banjos emanating from the woods across the street. The finances of the school also plummeted, and to make up the tuition gap, the school began taking on a disproportionate number of students who had been expelled from public schools, establishing an undercurrent of vice ranging from pot to pills, and even a sixteen-year-old eighth-grader who had caused one of the star cheerleaders to hemorrhage.

Marlon said they were better off walking around Bluff Park collecting deposit bottles and blowing their loot at Wizard's Palace, spending the afternoon playing Dig Dug or Tron. At least they would go home and not have to worry about whether or not they were going to JDC or some kind of bullshit like that—live their lives like criminals and worry all the goddamn time. "We go to the school, we burn it down, or we don't go at all," he said. "We can siphon some gas from the lawnmower at my house. We don't need much. Get the gas, we go."

Jackson pointed to a snout poking out from beneath a rock in the small pool where the drain emptied. "That's a bullfrog," he said. "Get it," he said to Fisher.

Jackson pointed to a spot where one of the rocks jutted out at the bottom, with a small crevice covered with algae. It was difficult for any of them to determine whether what Jackson saw was a rock or one of the bullfrogs. Fisher said if he wanted a bullfrog so bad, he could get it himself.

Jackson said he couldn't believe that he had friends that

were such cowards and removed his socks and shoes, stepped in the water, and caught his balance on a piece of sandstone that crumbled to the touch, sinking Jackson immediately to his knees, muck halfway up his shins. Heightening his embarrassment, when Jackson looked up, behind Marlon and Fisher, he saw the open passenger-side window of his uncle Runner's Pontiac Sun Bird Sport Coupe.

"What are you idiots doing?" the voice said from inside the Pontiac.

"Catching bullfrogs," Fisher said.

Jackson told Fisher to shut it and climbed out of the muck.

"Come on," Runner said. "Get in the car."

"What for?" Jackson said.

Runner stepped from the car and approached the three boys, Jackson's feet covered in black and green. "Wash those feet before getting in the car."

Jackson stepped back in the water and shook his feet. Runner told him to cut the crap, and forced Jackson into a sitting position and scooped water onto Jackson's shins, rubbing the grime from his feet and between his toes. Runner stepped back to the car and took a towel from the trunk and wiped Jackson's feet dry. "Now, get in the car. All of you."

"What did I do?" Jackson said. "Did mom send you to pick me up?"

"There's a fight at the church," Runner said. "It's going to be big."

"Our church?" Jackson said.

"No. The Baptist church. Andy Moseman is fighting some guy that used to go to your school. We gotta get there before it starts. We have to see this thing."

Runner pulled a three-point turn and took off towards Savoy, passing Jackson's house on the back way to John's Convenience

Store to pick up a pack of cigarettes. When he got back in the car, he packed his cigarettes and said that somebody at the fight was going to have a chain. That's what he heard. It could be Moseman. It could be the other guy.

"What kind of chain?" Fisher said.

"I don't' know," Runner said. "A *chain*."

"A bike chain?"

"Who cares?" Jackson said.

"Not a bike chain," Runner said. "Just a chain. Don't worry about it."

Marlon said that the Bible says that if you attack a country, you should destroy every single person in the country. You have to have a total cleanse. Otherwise, the war goes on forever.

Runner said they weren't going to see a war. They were going to see a fight.

"You still don't show up to a fight with a chain. What is the person going to do with the chain? Is he going to kill the other guy?"

"Probably," Runner said. "Why else would you bring a chain? Why else would we go see it?"

Fisher said if you hit someone with a chain, the other person could just grab it and pull you closer.

Marlon said if you bring anything to a fight, you bring a gun. If it comes to it, you kill the other person. Otherwise, don't bring anything. But if you beat somebody with a chain, that person, and their friends, and their parents, and their children, and their children's children, are going to come back and exact revenge a hundredfold. You bring a chain, you win one fight, but the rest of your life is misery.

"Who are these guys?" Runner asked out loud to the three in the back, then hit the gas and drove toward the Baptist church.

Runner was ten years younger than Jackson's mother, almost young enough to look like her son. Runner had dropped out of high school after getting his girlfriend pregnant and had started working at a sheet-metal factory in Bessemer. He used to show up at Jackson's house regularly for dinner. After his girlfriend had the baby removed and left him, Runner showed up less frequently and usually unannounced. When he did show up, he brought barbecue or a bag of hamburgers from Jack's and would talk about how much he loved his job as a sheet-metal worker. He told Jackson's family that he was going to go into sales once he put his time in. Sheet metal was big business. He told Jackson's family sheet metal was his calling. He told them he knew this to be true when he first saw fresh stacks of aluminum slabs, and they shined so clear and alive that he ran his hands across the surface, and it was like the metal had spoken to him in secret code transmitted through his fingertips. He told them that when aluminum is molten, it does not glow like iron or steel, but holds its color. Jackson noticed that his uncle's eyes watered as he talked about this world. Runner said that he was not sure why, but this trait in an element was a thing to admire, and the smelting process is so hot and smoky and oppressive that you cannot imagine anything so beautiful emerges. He sat up and told Jackson's family that he didn't even feel normal unless it's a thousand degrees and he's dripping with sweat.

After dinner, Runner showed Jackson how to smoke pot. He told Jackson it was the best education you could get, but Jackson was unsure of whether Runner was referring to the weed or the aluminum.

"It's simple, and it's everything," Runner said. "You don't learn it from school, and you don't learn it from pussy. You almost learn it from pussy, but pussy burns you. It's this. This is what I am talking about," but Jackson was still unsure about what 'this' thing was; he felt as if a layer of film had been placed between his mind and his thoughts, and all he could think about was terror. He thought about botulism and wild dogs, and all the accidents at the plant Runner had told him about. Stifling heat and smoke, fingers snipped like putty, thumbs and raw skull against sharp edges and unmovable objects, whole patches of skin peeled from forearms and faces, the sight of raw bone. The filter in Jackson's psyche, the film, remained fixed, and Jackson wondered if he would ever come down, or if this was just the new him.

At the Baptist church, cars had lined up around the perimeter, and a crowd had gathered in the middle of the parking lot like a rock festival. People walked around without aim, girls wearing concert shirts, tits on all of them. The crowd grew dense at the middle, but it was impossible to tell who was fighting, or if the people fighting were in their respective camps, or if they had even arrived. All three of the boys felt the tension of some great possibility. Many of the teenagers walked on tiptoes, straining to look over the heads of their peers, also trying to figure out who was where, and what was going to happen, and Runner told the three boys to climb a tree or stay around the edges. Just get a good place to watch and stay out of the way. Somebody had already ambled up the angled concrete supports of the church, and crawled monkey-style up the rooftop at sixty degrees, all along the tiles to the apex, where the church suggested a steeple, but now featured a late teen in blue jeans, hands gripping the peak and legs dangling over the edge.

A couple of teenagers told the boys to stand on the hood of their car, a 1971 Dodge Dart, and the view opened up before them. Two cars, a sky-blue Chevy Nova and rusted-out red Volkswagen Rabbit, had been parked in the center of the crowd, forming an impromptu pit. More girls in concert shirts.

31

More tits. Moccasin boots laced all the way up with fritters. But then the crowd parted, and a tall preppie walked to the center. Marlon knew him from the way he walked, a slight bow in his legs. Nelson Hadley, the goalie of their varsity soccer team. State champ. Nelson had been a part of the exodus after the burning of worldly goods. Marlon recalled a moment during the bonfire, where Jimbo Parsons had emptied a sack of worldly goods onto the heap before the pile was ignited, including a can of beer he had drained on the way to school and a porno. The leaves of the magazine had flapped open, and Marlon remembered catching a quick glimpse of a blonde woman on her knees, hands tied behind her back while she performed fellatio on a man painted purple with an oversized helmet, looking part spaceman, part light bulb. Marlon remembered Nelson, too, taking offense to this and getting in Jimbo Parson's face, demanding to know exactly what Jimbo wanted to accomplish. Participate, or stay home, he shouted at Jimbo Parsons. *Participate* or stay home. This is not a game. This is not entertainment.

Nelson Hadley was considered by the students at their school, as well as the coaches and most of the parents, to be a true athlete. Once, during the semi-finals of the state soccer tournament, with the game on the line, the opposing team had kicked a corner. The ball veered way out to the edge of the penalty box, then turned inward. While players from opposing teams jumped to head the ball either direction, the figure of Nelson Hadley's torso had risen above the players, scooping the ball to his chest, then somersaulting over the shoulders of his opponents, careless of whose head and feet and elbows might be out for him, then landed on his back, tightening into a fetal position, before rising and booting the ball deep into enemy territory. He spat a wad of blood to the ground. Marlon remembered seeing the blood bounce off the dusty surface of the soccer field, reflecting in the afternoon sun like a discarded jewel. Game over. Nelson Hadley also pitched Pony League baseball, ran cross-country, and had placed two consecutive years in the Vulcan Run. Now, he danced on bare feet with the sleeves of his Izod royal blue velour shirt pulled up to his elbows.

"Look at that," Fisher said to Marlon and Thomas, pointing to two people standing next to a green Kawasaki dirt bike. One of them stood tall, taller than Nelson Hadley. Marlon said the next guy, the small guy, was Andy Moseman, who was crazy. Small and stocky. Marlon looked at his friends and said that Moseman lived two blocks over, and once he saw Moseman getting high from the fumes of his bike. Marlon told the others that he had seen him in his driveway, staring at his grandmother, who watched him from their front porch while he huffed gasoline straight from the tank of his motorcycle, the siphon held to a single nostril until he passed out. Other things were common knowledge about Andy Moseman. He had fallen from the bluffs on Shades Crest Road, fifty feet to granite, cushioned by a layer of autumn leaves, only to get up and walk away with a chipped tooth. He had been hit by a car, and made the papers two years before after he had beaten up the father of two girls in the Skate World parking lot.

Moseman walked towards the parking lot with his helmet on, his eyes shaded by a black visor. His stocky frame waddled, swinging his hips awkwardly as he walked—his feet, in a pair of blue and yellow Nike LDVs, moved faster than his body. As he approached the pit and the two cars, he removed his helmet. Moseman's shoulder-length hair fell out, framing a face impossibly packed with pimples—ridges and inflammation clear and defined from fifty yards away, a face pulsing and bulging with pus. Moseman held the helmet his with his right hand, then brought it down hard against Nelson Hadley's extended forearm. The crowd surged forth and turned into a sound of collective awe, terror and glee, while Moseman's arm swung with machine like precision, rapid fire, knocking down Nelson's arm and connecting with Nelson's orbital bone, driving him to the ground. The boys wondered if the blows had killed Hadley. He had fallen backward, and his head bounced on the pavement. Both of his arms raised in a slight begging position, as if his nerves had taken over.

The crowd reminded Marlon of the scene of the bonfire, the same intensity. He remembered seeing Pastor Vincent walking along the outskirts of the scene, his suppressed joy at Newschannel 6's appearance, and the regional attention the event would garner. Marlon could see Pastor Vincent formulating a sermon in his mind at that very moment. People would jeer, people would ridicule them for their righteousness. Let them. First purification, then longsuffering. If people wanted to laugh, let them laugh. If people wanted to mock, let them mock.

However, later that day, after the burning, the look over Pastor Vincent's face had changed, and he had visited each individual classroom to speak his mind. He spoke to the students with frankness at his horror that morning, shuffling through their objects of worldly goods before dousing them with lighter fluid. "The level of your stumbling is frightening," Pastor Vincent had said to them. "Abhorrent. Prophylactics. Cigarettes. Rock albums. *Play*boy." Pastor Vincent looked at the classroom and seemed to make eye contact with each student simultaneously. "What troubles me is that you don't even know what you did today. My fear is that those who will mock us will be none other than yourselves."

Moseman turned around and faced the crowd of teenagers and grabbed himself. However, Hadley came to. The boys saw him vomit, then get to his knees and take in his surroundings.

Blood covered the side of Hadley's face and neck, but still, he raised himself to his feet, and it was not until that point that he appeared to be aware of the situation, and the blood coating his face and neck, blackening his royal blue velour shirt, was his own. Somehow, he stood, but before he could land a punch to the side of Moseman's turned head, he was pulled back by a rush of teenagers, who slammed him against the side of the sky-blue Chevy Nova. His velour shirt came apart in strips, and the boys saw that the blood and had soaked through to his torso as well. In the pocket of mayhem, the boys saw Runner make a move forward, delivering a few lightning fast body blows of his own to Nelson's ribs, followed by an open handed slap to the face. That's when the boys saw that Runner was right, Moseman did have a chain, a thin chain, five or so feet in length, designed as a dog leash. Moseman wrapped the chain around his hand like a whip, striping Hadley's back and shoulders, until the crowd was upon them, dense and pressing, then popped loose like wild atoms, punctured with the modulating pulse of a squad car.

That night, Marlon awoke to a scraping sound in his room. A soft grind, slowly scratched, as if someone stood in the dark dragging the edge of a sheet of typing paper against the surface of his dresser drawer. The sound stopped, and just before he re-entered his slumber, the sound picked up again. It was difficult for him to tell if the aural image resulted from a cockroach or a mouse, but the timbre struck a nerve that allowed neither sleep nor proper relaxation. The sound seemed to Marlon bigger than a cockroach but smaller than a mouse or a rat. The sound stopped again, but he had awoken. He looked at the ceiling and could see colors swirling in his vision, greens and yellows, and orange and red and a flare of bright orange dots that shifted from defined patterns to a blur. When he closed his eyes, he found himself thinking about Nelson Hadley and replayed the scene in his mind from that afternoon. Marlon wondered if maybe Nelson was dead, maybe he was in a coma. He wanted to ask his parents if they had heard anything on the news but knew that question would lead to many other questions. He closed his eyes again and imagined Nelson at Parisian's walking around with his parents, trying on Izod velours. Marlon imagined Nelson's mother giving him a burgundy sweater, telling him to try it on, then handing him the same one in green, and then blue, then trying a size larger, then a size smaller, and his mother asking the salesperson fold the sweater in white tissue inside the cardboard box. But it probably didn't happen like that at all. Nelson's mother probably bought the velour sweater for him while he was at school without even mentioning it to him. She probably just brought home the shirt and hung it up in his closet. Who knows, Marlon thought. It could have been hanging there for weeks.

HOME FRIES

It was odd. The beaded curtain at Our Place Café was colorful from the dining room but black and garish from the kitchen view, even with the sun shining through. You would have thought it would be the opposite. The beads themselves gave the room an unnatural feel, matched with the wall-to-wall office carpet. Ficus by the entrance. Hippy décor versus motel lobby. Miranda, my boss, had already set each table with napkin-wrapped silverware, bowls of slaw, sliced bread, and little tabs of butter. Even the smells in the dining room seemed to be at odds, warm bread clashing with disinfectant and pockets of funk that proliferated in all kinds of unpredictable spots in restaurants. Grime.

I stood at the front window of Our Place Café with the cook, Fat Sam, and we looked at an angle down University Avenue for festivities. A city parade was scheduled for late morning, but outside, the police had yet to clear vehicles and pedestrians from the road, although pylons and sawhorses had been set up next to side streets so they could block it off when necessary. Signs up on the lampposts and parking meters let people know their cars would be towed at the owner's expense.

Fat Sam's belly hung so low that his apron seemed more like some kind of abdominal bra. He had shaved his nickname in the back of his head: Fat Sam. He had been training me for kitchen prep, coring cabbages, dicing carrots into matchsticks, mixing up dressing and tubs of coleslaw.

"A parade," Fat Sam said, and had said several times already, as if the concept were new to me, or as if we were about to witness some grand conjunction of planets seen every thousand years. He told me there were going to be customers in droves. He said vehicles would pass that would be covered in decorations, trucks with platforms like pirate ships and covered wagons. People on these vehicles would throw candy and all kinds of trinkets to the crowds.

"Like a parade," I said.

Fat Sam looked at me.

"What?" I said.

"Come on," he said, motioning me back to the kitchen. He had two metal tubs of scrambled eggs keeping warm on the back side of the griddle. We had bread in every phase of preparation placed around the kitchen. Bowls of dough rising under towels, dough shaped into loaves, loaves baking in the oven, loaves cooling on racks. We had a pot of potatoes for home fries cooling on the center steel countertops. The smell in the kitchen, however, was so dense with flavors and pungent with yeast, fermentation, and thick with butter, bacon and eggs that it didn't even make you feel hungry. You felt full. So full you wanted to crawl under a crate and take a nap, fold up your apron and take a trip to REM-stage Tahiti, toes in the sand with an umbrella poking out of your piña colada, Fat Sam sitting next to you testing the tension on his Rubbermaid beach lounger, telling you the sky was blue because particles in space absorbed all other parts of the spectrum, sand was round due to eons of pulverization, water was less salty near the shoreline and every other obvious thing you could think of. Fat Sam broke my musing and told me to hurry up. The parade was coming soon.

Miranda, my boss, also owned Our Place Café. She was pretty, but restaurant work was churning her into premature middle age. Twenty-eight going on forty-five. Miranda was convinced the parade was going to save her business. I had only known her for less than a full day, but already I could understand that the parade was all she talked about. Even the day before, when she had hired me as an emergency fill-in, she told me she and Fat Sam could swing things themselves, but not during a parade. And the parade was going to be big. The parade was going to get her out of debt. The parade was going to establish the café as the go-to morning eatery along the strip. The parade was going to give her the upward momentum to establish herself with some pull at the Chamber of Commerce. The parade was equal to five thousand dollars worth of advertisement, and the allotted advertising money she could pour into the business, maybe build an outside dining area behind the café. The parade was going to get her dad and husband off her back. The parade, the parade, the parade.

I didn't want to say anything but, privately, I wondered if a parade would bring in any real business. After all, parades move along the street, and people move along with them. If anything, you would need to set up tables outside the café to give people a chance to soak it all in, but the city had cleared the sidewalks of all obstruction. Or at least serve samples from one of the floats and scatter coupons like confetti. In my estimation, people move along with parades and then go home. They don't return to any of the places they might have seen along the way. People might make a mental note, but they probably make mental notes all along the way and then just forget everything. After all, most of the people at the parade would be drunk, or have to buy groceries after, or a zillion other things to think about besides her café. I didn't want to say anything to Miranda, though, since she seemed to be all caught up in her delusion. Besides, she seemed nice, and it would be good working for a nice boss—I had not experienced that before, and I was curious.

In a way, the place had already begun to feel like family.

The job at Our Place had saved me. I had quit school and moved to Gainesville to play music and, after two weeks, I was already broke. Not busted, but teetering. I had been promised a job at Schoolkids Records on University Avenue, but upon arrival the manager, an old friend from home, had succumbed to selective amnesia and left me beating the pavement a mile and a half up University Avenue, turning my hand into a claw filling out job applications all the way up. Do you have any experience? *No.* May we contact your former employees? What days are you available? Are you in school? How do you see your skills functioning in a working environment? Can you thrive in stressful conditions? Where do you see yourself in five years?

It got so bad that all of my thoughts and attention had begun to funnel down to finances. Thirty dollars for electricity. Twenty-five for phone. Fifteen for gas. Seven for groceries. When my roommate, Charles Russell, and I had moved in, our landlord had given us a month free, and I had money for the second month, but we had grossly underestimated the cost of cleaning supplies and utility connection fees. I was down to a handful of cash for burritos and Milwaukee's Best, and scraping together two hundred dollars by the end of the next month seemed like an impossibility. I even stopped by the Gainesville Plasma Center for testing and was awaiting word on the salability of my platelets. Ten dollars the first pint, fifteen the second pint.

After my third week of futility, I spent a dollar-ten on a cup of coffee at Our Place Café and sat next to the front window to get down with some Fante. *Ask the Dust.* Ah, Bandini. Where's my Hackmuth? Of course, there she was, and her name was Miranda. She refilled my coffee and said she was the owner of the café. Was I new in town? Did I need a job? The following morning there would be a parade, and she needed an emergency fill-in. Could I start at six? I can wait until six, no problem, I told her. Six in the morning, she said.

Fat Sam said we still needed a tub of potato salad, and we could save the sausages for last, but we didn't want to wait too long. You leave one thing out, and before you know it, a party of fifty comes in and all they want is the thing that you haven't got. We run out of food during a parade, that is a mark, he reminded me. Fat Sam set the tubs of eggs and bacon on the stainless-steel countertop, squirted a line of corn oil on the grill, then scraped along the surface a pumice brick that grated and tore at your tympanic membrane. Then he dumped a bucket of water on the surface, creating a mushroom cloud of steam, leaving water marbles dancing on the grill until they shrank into pellets and tiny silver grains. Then he squirted more oil and heaped on cups of chopped onions, shaping the pile until they turned translucent and produced a deep smell of caramel. Fat Sam carved and shaped as if he were listening to music in his head, and then he dumped on a tub of chopped potatoes. He cut a quarter of a bread loaf and stuffed the entire piece in his mouth, then cut off another quarter and tossed it to me. When he worked down the bread, he told me that a critic was coming out to the café. He was going to do a write-up in the *Alligator*. "If he can fight the crowd," he said.

"Why's a critic going to be at a parade?" I said.

"Why not?" Fat Sam said. "Everyone's going to be here." He said he wished his kids could be there, too, but they couldn't be running around the kitchen while he was working. "You have any kids?"

"One," I said. "My roommate. He's twenty-one and worthless." I thought Fat Sam would laugh, but instead he just told me he had three kids. Three boys. "Three expensive boys," he said, then asked if I was making enough money.

"No," I said, except that I had an appointment for selling my plasma down the road.

"You sell your blood?"

"Plasma."

"What the hell is plasma?"

"It's the fluid that your hemoglobin swims around in."

"Hemoglobin?"

"Your red blood cells."

"I know what hemoglobin is. Don't you need that shit?"

"Of course. That's why they pay you."

Fat Sam reached down and turned the heat up on the home fries, then squirted a zig-zag of corn oil on the potatoes and re-shaped them. He told me that some people believe that your soul is in your blood, and I told him that some people believe that the moon is made of blue cheese.

"Listen," he said, and told me that if I was hard up for money, he knew a friend who could hook me up with people in Starke County where you can make fifty dollars for taking part in executions. They hire three people to pull the switch. Only one switch was hooked up, so none of the executioners know who does the job. "Fifty bucks each," he said, "but one person does the job. I can hook you up if you're interested."

"Fifty dollars to kill someone," I said.

"You don't know if it's you. Besides, it's not killing someone. You're executing somebody. You're performing a service," he said. He took a tub of sausages from the refrigerator and dumped the heap on the griddle, then spread out the links. "If you don't do it, someone else is going to do it. It's just like a machine."

It seemed as if it happened in a moment, but outside the street emptied, and pedestrians walked casually along the pavement ignorant of the white-and-yellow lines, and then they disappeared. In a flash, the first float appeared. From our vantage point in the kitchen, all you could see were black or blue pants and the bottoms of wheelchairs, but you got the idea that they might have been veterans of the Korean War, or maybe even World War II, and then the next float had a bunch of naked legs that you assumed belonged to bikini girls from their high school surf club, or maybe a sorority from the university, all dancing about because they were outside and you were inside. And then Fat Sam was right: a covered wagon.

And then there was a float that had an actual lion. It was a real lion, but caged, in a little circus box with iron bars, and the lion was either sedated, stuffed with giraffe meat, or smart enough to stay calm and wait for his chance. I had actually seen the lion two days earlier on the bike ride out to Schoolkids Records when I had cut through the woods behind the veterinary college. I assumed it was the same lion as the parade, because it looked the same. The beast I had seen had been in a similar cage, locked up outside. It was surprising and came as a shock that the lion was not under any kind of guard. I was able to ride up to it and press my face right against the bars and look directly into its eyes. Either way, watching the parade gave me a blue feeling. All of that manufactured joviality.

The chime on the front door sounded, and Fat Sam said they were coming in, the rush was going to start, but it was only Miranda going outside to assess the situation. It sounded again, and again Fat Sam and I bit, but it was just her coming back inside. It happened a third time, but after that we just understood it was Miranda, and Fat Sam tossed me another wedge of bread.

I had to admit, Fat Sam's offer sounded interesting. In the previous two afternoons I had exhausted every foreseeable opportunity, getting the same spiel from managers at the donut shop, burger shop, pizza shop, book shop, yogurt shop, art-supply shop. The Holiday Inn was promising with a possible gig as a banquet waiter, but I needed thirty dollars to put down for a used tuxedo. I wondered if Fat Sam were telling the truth, if it were that easy to make fifty bucks up in Starke. I wondered how often they hired people to throw the switch, and if it would be enough to really supplement my income, and I wondered if it were really a switch. But, certainly, it made sense that they would hire nobodies to carry out the executions. The judge would not want to have taken the trouble of going to law school, work his whole life to rise to the thronehood of judge, only to slink back down to the role of executioner. And it wouldn't be a bailiff, either—they didn't sign up for that. Nobody is going to pull the switch unless they absolutely had to. But I thought about it. I thought if it were a one-shot deal, I could take my chance. If it was a firing range, it would be easy. When the officer yelled "Fire!" I would hesitate. If the man crumpled, I'd pull the trigger. If he didn't, then I would hold my fire. But if it were a switch, then you wouldn't be able to game the system, and God knows I would be the one with the juice. I could not have that. I would spend the rest of my life having forgotten all about it, or trying to forget about it, then at the end of the line make it to Final Judgment, and I would have a death on my hands. That was a mortal sin. No way that was going to work. Either that, or they would find out twenty years later through DNA testing or some found document that my man was innocent after all, and then I would transform from killer to murderer, and I couldn't have that either. But fifty dollars. I asked Fat Sam if he had ever taken part in the executions.

"Oh, hell no," he said.

"Why not?"

"Because I ain't no killer."

"*I* ain't no killer," I said.

"Sure." He told me he didn't think I was. I didn't look like a killer. On the other hand, he said white people had fewer hangups about killing people, so he thought he would mention it.

"Black people kill all the time," I said.

"True, but white people justify your murders. Black people do it and know it's wrong. White people murder and think it's okay if they got a good enough reason. Like this. Like ... executions. White people are always looking for an excuse to kill someone if the reason is right. Somebody said Vietnam was all about an idea."

"You have drive-bys," I said.

"I don't drive-by."

"You don't," I said, "but I don't drop napalm on villagers."

Fat Sam said that either way it was the same thing. If I was interested, then I was interested; if I wasn't interested, then I wasn't interested. All he wanted to do was give me a hand.

When the parade had passed, Miranda was still outside, and Fat Sam had me washing dishes, pots and pans, then scrubbing the grease traps, which were impossible. You can't clean grease traps. The grease evaporates from the griddle and cakes up on the metal filters and turns into a kind of gluey goo. Like sap. And you cannot wash it off. You can wash it with hot water, wash it with detergent, wash it in cold water and take to it with steel wool, and you can run it through the machine as many times as you want, but the grease holds fast to the metal filter. In fact, it hardens. Its molecular grip tightens. After a time, I noticed Fat Sam watching me clean the traps, and he told me to give him the goddamned grease traps, that you aren't supposed to clean them to a tee, just clean them enough to pass inspection.

"Come on, man!" he said. "Toss me the traps."

I asked him if there was maybe going to be another parade, and he said there were not going to be any other goddamned parades. How many parades did I think they had?

Miranda paid me cash for the day. She could pay me five dollars per hour for seven hours, and she threw in an extra ten, which I assumed was a severance package. On the ride home from Our Place Café, the town snapped back in to form, as if the parade was just some kind of half-spoiled food it had to pass before feeling normal again. Even on my bicycle, I still smelled of scrambled eggs, funk and bread. I bypassed Archer Road and cut back on 34th Street to the shortcut behind the veterinary school. I was hoping that maybe I could see that lion again. Miranda had also paid me in food. I had a backpack full of bread, quarts of potato salad, a square plastic container stuffed with scrambled eggs and bacon, and one Ziploc bag of sausages. I knew the lion would like sausages, no doubt. Cooked or raw. Maybe if he were there I could toss him a few, see what kind of kick that beast still had in him. If he liked the sausages, I would let him try the other stuff. I had a half gallon of potato salad, and that stuff goes rank PDQ. Maybe he would like it. Maybe not. But of course, this time, as I rode along the dirt trail between the woods and the veterinarian college, the lion was no longer there. What had I expected to see?

ALL EIGHTY-EIGHT KEYS

Kessinger caught up with Tag on the way home from school, kicking up the rear wheel of his Diamondback Turbolight and spraying him with gravel. Tag jumped back, nearly impaling himself on a Spanish bayonet plant, then relaxed when he saw that it was Kessinger. Tag knew that this was Kessinger's way of greeting people he liked, and thus took no offense, though he wished Kessinger might develop a less informal introduction.

"Hey," Kessinger said. "We have to find a spot at the Pit. I know some girls who fuck."

Tag looked at Kessinger with some hesitation, still parsing through the fear of having his fourteen-year-old body plucked from the swords of a yucca plant, and said that there were plenty of places at the Pit.

"We need a spot for us," Kessinger said. "We have to find a place to put a mattress."

"We're going to drag a mattress to the Pit?" Tag said.

"Don't fret," Kessinger said. He told Tag that they could probably use sleeping bags if they couldn't get a mattress, but that wasn't the point.

"You think they'll do it with us?" Tag said. "The girls."

"They'll do it with me, I know. They were talking about it at school." Kessinger motioned for Tag to stand on the bolts of his back wheel, and they rode towards Tag's house on Montclair. Kessinger slowed to look for traffic at the intersection of Highland and Keene, then said, "They were talking about guys who they'd fuck in class, and they said me. My sister told me. She heard them. Melinda Everett and Stephanie Davidson. They said they would fuck me."

Tag knew of Stephanie Davidson, and he had heard about Melinda Everett. Melinda had been a big deal a couple of years earlier. At the time, she had been the second youngest person to survive a heart transplant. She had been in the *St. Pete Times*. Dunedin Middle School had staged a small parade in her honor when she came home from the hospital after five months of waiting for a compatible organ.

When they got to the ballpark across the street from Tag's neighborhood, they stopped for a cigarette on the aluminum bleachers. "The girls said they would do it with you, not me," Tag said.

"Don't worry, Fat Pat can get us some Wild Turkey. They'll fuck you."

"Fat Pat," Tag said. Fat Pat's face was covered with, not so much pimples, as lesions, and there seemed to be always on his skin a weeping sore of some sort—transparent gel that looked like his body had been genetically modified to produce honey. Fat Pat was also famous at school for his ability to score liquor. "I don't know about Fat Pat," Tag said.

"Don't be a pussy," Kessinger said. "Fat Pat'll get us some whiskey. They'll fuck you."

The Pit was an undeveloped subdivision with an electric power station on the western perimeter and lemon groves to the south. The land spread out with sandy trails between brush, palmetto bushes, and ponytail pines. Wild watermelon vines snaked among the concrete pipes and the occasional stray bulldozer, or stacks of metal frames and cinder blocks, as if contractors continually tinkered with the notion of erecting a neighborhood. Tag and Kessinger had once found a foot-long amphibious creature flapping in an abandoned sewer pipe that appeared to be part eel, part catfish, part snake. Two rectangular reservoirs of gray sludge acted as a moat around the power station that Tag thought might be quicksand. The teenagers rarely ventured into the lemon groves, though rumor had it that a body had once been found there.

There were hot spots, too, at the Pit—nooks tucked away, where high-schoolers had laid out mattresses and left behind empty cases of beer and liquor bottles, used condoms and empty sandwich bags. Tag had once found a Van Halen concert shirt with a lion emerging from the graphics and thought about taking it home, but the fabric had been overtaken by mold and gunk.

Had Tag been pressed to pinpoint a word, he would have used revere, admire, or respect, but more accurately, Tag was enamored of Kessinger. Kessinger had the rare ability to turn every aberration or defect into cool. Kessinger did nothing to hide the cow-lick parting his hair wildly to each side. Rather, he combed his hair in a fashion accentuating his cow-lick. Kessinger even walked with a slight, bow-legged limp, as if he had suffered a minor bout of polio when he was a child, but he carried the gait with a stroll, as if he were approaching a fistfight. When Kessinger smiled, the right side of his mouth tipped down at an angle, giving everything he said, or every facial expression, no matter how genuine, a tinge of sarcasm. Kessinger could ride wheelies all the way down the street on his Turbolite, bunny hop onto park benches, and do wall-rides that made him look as if he defied gravity for nearly a full second, and he kicked beer cans into oncoming traffic with his rear wheel. He performed tricks as an afterthought, as a sort of tic, but if anyone ever requested a trick, he would simply allow his mouth to tip down at an angle, then raise a silent middle finger.

Stephanie and Melinda were sitting on beach towels in Stephanie's driveway listening to a jam box set on a wooden barstool. The girls wore bikinis, and from several houses away, Tag could see the outline of Stephanie's rib cage. Melinda wore a blue T-shirt with the sleeves cut off. Duran Duran played on the radio, and when they pulled up, Stephanie looked at Kessinger and said, "Hey, fag."

"I'll show you *fag*," he said.

Tag noticed that this was the exact opposite reaction that he would have had. Where he would have responded with *defense*, Kessinger chose *engagement*.

"Hey, you," Stephanie said to Tag. "You're friends with Kessinger?"

The sun had begun to descend above the houses, and the girls stood up and stepped into shorts. They each kept the top button of their shorts undone, with bikini triangles still visible. Tag wondered if Melinda had worn the T-shirt to hide her scar. It seemed as if she had removed as much fabric as possible without exposing the space six inches below and above her sternum. The sleeves had been ripped off at the neckline, and the bottom half of the T-shirt had been torn into strips.

Once, when Tag stayed home sick from school, he had watched a program on PBS that showed an open-heart surgery. They had shown the entire procedure. The woman's torso had shone white under the lamps, and the doctors slathered her skin with iodine solution and sawed the sternum right down the middle, pried the bones apart, creating a sound akin to branches snapping from a tree. Tag glanced at Melinda again, and she was looking at him. He fumbled a cigarette from his pocket—crushed and bent, only marginally smokeable.

"You smoke?" Stephanie said.

"Yeah," Tag said.

"Yeah?" Kessinger said. "You don't smoke."

"I smoke sometimes in my room," Tag said. "Sometimes."

"You're sometimes Franken Spanky in your room."

"Got any more cigarettes?" Melinda said.

"At home. I do at home."

"Gimme a drag," Kessinger said, taking the cigarette. He supported his weight with one foot on the ground and the other on a pedal and dragged the cigarette deep, blowing smoke in a clean line before it blossomed into a cloud between the four of them. Kessinger nodded at the girls. "Invite my buddy over here to talk to some chicks, and the motherfucker brings over a Winston. *One cig*," he said, and the three laughed.

Stephanie took the cigarette and dragged as if an afterthought and said that they had just missed the two guys who were there. A couple of missionaries. Two guys who looked identical. Same hair, same pants, same shoes, same skin, same ears, same everything, except one was about six-foot-three, and the other was barely taller than Melinda. And fat. But the tall one was hot. The shorter one would have been hot, too, if he had not been so short and fat, and schoolboyish.

Kessinger said that he should have been there to kick their asses, and Melinda kicked his tire and said that you can't kick a missionary's ass.

"Did they try to scam on you?" Kessinger said.

"They didn't try to scam on us. They were deep, actually." Stephanie said. "He kept talking about piano keys."

"The handsome one or the fat one?" Kessinger said.

"The tall one," Melinda said.

"They were trying to scam," Kessinger said, nodding at Tag.

"What did he say?" Melinda said.

"He said that before, he understood life, but it was like he could make music on only twenty keys," Stephanie said. "Now he can make music on all eighty-eight keys. Isn't that beautiful?"

"I need a book to hold in front of my pants," Kessinger said.

"You're a jerk," Stephanie said.

Melinda said that the tall one was probably nineteen. The short one was the same age. Maybe eighteen, maybe twenty. Kessinger asked if that wasn't too old for them, and Stephanie said that twenty was too old, but eighteen wasn't. They should ask a professional, she said, nodding at Melinda. "When Melinda, here, was nine, she let a guy eat her out in the garage. He was twice her age." Stephanie said that the guy had been walking past the garage while Melinda was dancing to the radio, and minutes later he sat her down on her dad's weight bench. "Can you believe this girl?"

It was hard for Tag to tell if Stephanie was making up the story or not, but the details carried a tone of authenticity—the weight bench, the drawstring, the cardboard box and the fumes from an overturned bottle of green rubbing alcohol, and the paramour's age—nineteen.

Tag's hands dampened on his bicycle grips. The sun had settled over the stucco houses, the yucca plants and lemon trees, the cacti, clay-tiled roofs, the St. Augustine grass, plagued with mounds of fire ants. Tag asked if they had ever caught the man.

"Where'd you pick up this one?" Stephanie said to Kessinger. "He's a talker."

"He's *deep*," Kessinger said, then dragged, blew a line of smoke, and let the sides of his mouth tip down as he smiled.

The four agreed to hook up Saturday night at one. They would meet in Stephanie's driveway, then walk the five blocks to the Pit. There was no mention of what they would do once they got to the Pit, or who would match up with whom, or if there would be any matching up at all, but Tag could not imagine Kessinger not teaming up with one of them, and after that, he would be left to his own devices. They agreed that they would drink beer, and they would drink lots of it. Stephanie kicked Kessinger's wheel and said that they were going to get the missionaries drunk. *Shit*, Kessinger said. Shit, nothing, Stephanie said. The missionaries were going to show up, and she was going to get them drunk. She said they could mess with them, but they wanted to party. I'd lay a missionary, Stephanie said, then asked Melinda if she wouldn't lay a missionary, and Melinda said she would lay a missionary if she didn't have to lay a short, squat missionary that smelled like Aqua Velva. Stephanie said she wouldn't lay a missionary unless it *was* the fat one, and they both laughed.

Tag tried to let the palms of his hands air-dry in the moist Florida air, and Kessinger showed his muscles where he had once pressed the tip of a red-hot lighter on his deltoids. Tag tried to avoid eye contact with Melinda. Was this the same girl the doctors and nurses had stripped nude on a gurney, sawed down the middle and had her chest wall cracked open, tubes and wires hooked up, pumping and streaming with oxygen and fluid, sewed up and stitched with black twine? How could they have ripped apart a girl like this and kept her beauty so intact? Her eyes were enough.

On the ride home, just as they turned onto Union Street, Kessinger performed a spellbinding trick that caused his rear wheel to suddenly elevate, then turn sideways, running down the side of a wooden mailbox, forcing the post down at an angle, then slamming the wooden box to the ground with a dull thud. The faux-birdhouse did not shatter, but collapsed upon itself. The action was strictly perfunctory, followed by a total absence of acknowledgement or impulse to speed away. Instead, they stopped several houses further on at the intersection of Keene and Union and divvied up the responsibilities. Fat Pat lived down the street from Kessinger's, and all Tag needed to bring was one sleeping bag and a box of rubbers.

"What about the mattress?" Tag said.

"Fuck the mattress," Kessinger said. "What are we going to do, drag a mattress all the way down to the Pit? Shit," Kessinger said, and reminded Tag not to fuck it up, just to bring the rubbers. Tag asked if he should bring enough for the missionaries, and Kessinger flexed his right arm as if he were going to swing at Tag, then laughed. "Don't puss out," he said as he left, and then to make sure his point was clear, he shouted again, "Don't fret!"

Tag's youth group leader at church had warned the high-school group about premarital sex. They used all the scare tactics at church. They showed them videos and slide shows of herpes lesions, blackened penises, genital warts, bags of aborted babies, close-up images of bleeding sores, gaunt faces, and statistics of teenage suicide. The youth leaders told them that certain strains of VD could make your nerve endings so sensitive that taking off your clothes would feel like peeling off a layer of skin, and peeing was like a cocktail of urine, pus, and magma. They warned the teenagers that having sex before marriage would cause Christ to feel the pains of crucifixion all over again. "Why would you do that to somebody?" the youth minister had asked the group, then looked at Tag. "Because you're selfish, that's why."

The youth minister had once drawn up a chart, showing that if you slept with one person, then you had actually slept with every person they had slept with, and every person that person had slept with, then drew up a sort of Venn diagram of venereal diseases.

When Tag was certain that his parents had fallen asleep, thirty minutes after the blue television light had gone out, he loosened the screen from the window and lowered himself into the backyard. Once outside, he pondered the youth group leader's chart. He thought of the nineteen-year-old and Melinda, and the Petri dish of micro-vermin that man must have been carrying around. The math was dizzying, the scenes surreal. He thought of Stephanie servicing a fleet of missionaries—black pants wadded up all over her bedroom, white, short-sleeved dress shirts hanging from bedposts and door knobs, black combs and pens scattered about, a collection of magic underwear slung around her neck.

Once out of the neighborhood, the ride was easy. The air was cool, and he stayed in the shadows. He rode first to the 7-11 and pulled two boxes from the bathroom High-Class vending machine, then pulled off of Sunset Point and cruised through the neighborhoods. The ride felt good, and the wind cooled the air between his skin and the fabric of his polo shirt and shorts.

Recently, Tag had made a habit of sneaking out and riding his bicycle through the night streets of Clearwater. This was his world, free from centenarians, from Cadillacs and Oldsmobiles, silver foxes hogging the sidewalk with their golf carts. He felt safe, too. The weirdos were about in the daytime, lurking around the arcade for preteens jonesing for tokens, slobbering at the beach over bikini girls, drunk in the afternoon at JR's pizza shop. By late evening, the weirdos were either on the run, passed out or wading waist-deep in the mangroves of Tampa Bay, stuffing prostitutes into crab traps.

You could get some peace and quiet in the nighttime, and you could get some thinking done. Sneaking out had become his workshop, of sorts. He thought about recently, how he had been listening to *Diver Down*, and in his attempt to amplify the volume he had duplicated the cassette, then played the album on two jam boxes on opposite sides of the room. The music was not only louder, but after a brief moment, the sound of one cassette lagged just behind the other, creating a reverb effect. The music slowly evolved into echo, as if the band were playing live, right there in his bedroom, David Lee Roth, back in the band, rocking out like it was Tag's own private US Festival. The music changed again, the drums and guitars far out of sync, arrhythmic, loose and chaotic, as if an entirely new sound had been created. While Tag rode his bike through the Montclair Apartments toward Highland, he ruminated on his discovery, the possibility of recording normal sounds, everyday sounds, traffic, dishes, voices, and using them to mold his own sketches. This seemed like something, and the ruminations with the absence of Florida's standard heat oppression allowed him to feel lightheaded and alive.

When he reached Keene, he pulled a cigarette from his pocket and attempted to light it while riding, cupping the wind with his hands free from the wheel. He flicked the flint twice before the front wheel caught the space between the sidewalk and St. Augustine grass. His wheel buckled, his crotch just missed the base of the handlebars, and his legs entangled themselves in the bicycle frame. As he tried to regain his balance, his legs tangled further, and a moment later, he fell on his back, working himself free from the bicycle like a straitjacket.

Kessinger, Tag, and the two girls shotgunned two beers apiece. They pounded the beers. The missionaries had taken no time in building a fire. They had cleared out spaces for them to sit. Kessinger opened a pint of Wild Turkey and said, "Courtesy of Fat Pat." Tag drank the bourbon, smooth, and the whiskey burned and numbed his head when he inhaled. He passed the bottle to the girls, who each took a drink. The taller missionary, who had introduced himself as Micah, said that the shorter missionary, James, was such a goof that most people thought he was drunk all the time anyway. The last thing James needed was booze. Imagine what a goof he would be then.

"How cute," Kessinger said.

The teenagers positioned themselves equidistant from each other around the campfire, and the shadows of the palmetto bushes danced voodoo. The missionaries introduced themselves. Micah said he was from Los Angeles, and James said he was from Virginia. Kessinger asked them why they didn't just missionary where they lived, and Micah told them they needed to have the sensation of being displaced in order to free up their inhibitions.

Stephanie told Micah to tell the guys about his theory of the piano keys, and Micah laughed and said that it wasn't his theory, it was a way he himself had heard it explained.

"*Tell* them," Stephanie said.

Micah said it was no big deal that it was nothing really. It was just like having the ability to make meaning out of life. "Actually," he said, "it is a big deal, when you think about it. It's only your entire life. It's only eternity."

Kessinger started to talk, but Micah interrupted him and said, "Let me put it another way. When you see an individual impaired by drink, or drugs, the individual may feel the sensation of having another spirit take over their body, but what is really happening is that person has freed themselves from balance, law, and wisdom. Freedom of thought, too. They basically become animals. Shit, it's illegal to drive a car drunk, but people still feel the need to drive their bodies intoxicated. Imagine, steering your body towards eternity, drunk. That's a kind of insanity, if you think about it." Kessinger started to talk again, but again, Micah interrupted him. "You can have God at the controls, or you can have some dumb ass. Good luck with that," he said, smiling at James, then Stephanie. "I'm a heretic," Micah said. "I break things down into secular language. You can become superhuman, or you can *de*-humanize yourself. Which way do you want to go?"

"I told you they were deep," Stephanie said to Kessinger, picking up a small twig and tossing it his direction. Then Kessinger told everybody to watch, as he pulled a pint of Everclear from his backpack. He then removed a stick from the fire, swigged from the bottle and spat a ball of fire into the air; for that instant, the flames illuminated the faces of the missionaries, making them appear far older than the eighteen years they claimed.

The group settled in. Shotgunning beers had turned to sipping, and they talked. When the subject of Melinda's surgery came up, Stephanie told the missionaries that she had actually died for several minutes on the gurney. Melinda said it was three minutes. She had been dead for three minutes, and now she was alive with the heart of a total stranger.

Tag asked her if she had seen anything while she was gone.

"I wasn't gone. I was dead," she said.

Did she see a light?

"No," she said.

"You wouldn't see a light unless you had somebody shining the light for you," Micah said. "Otherwise you've got darkness. That's all you've got."

James said that he loved the fact that she had undergone a heart transplant. It was a real, physical representation of life's struggle. "It all goes back to the heart. You've actually exposed your heart for all to see. I think it's amazing."

"They think my man is a goof," Micah said, "but my man is profound." James sat with crossed legs on the sleeping bag, his hands folded and resting on his knees. His jaw occasionally jutted forth several inches, followed by a shifting shoulder beneath his skin, as if by means of faulty wiring or machinery. Tag noticed the precision of these intervals, and the action only ceased when Micah spoke.

The flames from the sticks settled into coals, and Stephanie announced that if the missionaries were not going to get drunk, they would have to agree to play games. They would go clockwise, then counterclockwise. Each could force their victim to chug a beer, take a shot, submit to a truth, or take a dare.

The readiness with which Micah and Kessinger kissed the girls was something that Tag could not wrap his head around. He wondered if he would be dared to kiss, and should this happen, if a spirit of some sort would descend and allow his muscles to perform actions by instinct. He tried not to watch too closely, but he could not avoid noticing a sudden looseness overtake Stephanie, as if all of her angles melted as Micah placed his hand under her breast, followed by the instinctive placing of her hand over his, pulling it up and onto her bosom, kneading her own breast with his hand. Kessinger's reaction seemed somehow opposite. When faced with kissing both Melinda and Stephanie, he froze, visibly calculating his approach, and rather than looking like a young man making out with girls, he looked like an older boy tiptoeing into no man's land. Kessinger and Micah also took turns with each girl in the burned-out school bus. They spent less time with Melinda and they took their time with Stephanie. When she returned with Kessinger, she appeared giddy, but when she returned with Micah, she seemed changed. She seemed different, and Tag noticed that when she sat next to the fire, her legs pulled up close to her chest, that her knees were shaking.

James looked at each of the teenagers carefully, as if his mind had already been made up, as if he were trying to conceal some deeply hidden fetish, settled on Melinda. He said, "Hi," and the single syllable seemed to startle her in the same manner as when the green wood in the fire occasionally dealt a swift and sudden blast of popping sap. James then dared Melinda to show the group her scar. Stephanie asked James if he thought she was lying, reminding him that she had been in the newspaper and even on television. "I just think it's powerful," he said. "We've all got our vulnerabilities," he said. "This is yours, and it's amazing. You can use it as inspiration. There's nothing ugly or grotesque about it at all, or even abnormal. It's a symbol of survival, of strength. New life. *That's* beauty."

"Should you?" Stephanie said to Melinda, and she said that she would. She had never thought about it like that, but it made sense. She had always been ashamed of it, but that's because they always talked about covering it up, or plastic surgery, but she had never thought of it the way James put it. She reached her arms back and unsnapped her bra, then unbuttoned her blouse, slowly spreading the fabric, just enough to display a nine-inch purple scar, dotted on each side with suture scars. Tag was surprised that from his angle, it took him nearly ten seconds before noticing that he could see a complete view of her left breast. James said that he would be honored if he could touch it. Tag felt heat rise to his scalp, and blood pulsed his ears. James sat next to Melinda, running an extended index finger south to north, then back down. "It's real," he said. "It's just beautiful." Melinda began to cry. Stephanie put her arm around her, and then without warning, she vomited. She threw up several times before violently dry heaving, her back arched. When she finished, she apologized and said that she wasn't drunk, it had just happened. She apologized again, washed her mouth with beer and spat it between her legs, then took a pull from the remaining beer and swallowed.

A silence fell on the group, and they listened to the music of tires meeting pavement on Union Street and Highland, the scurrying of vermin and the type of silence that is only possible in the dense Florida humidity, surrounded by wild plants and campfires. Micah thanked them for the invitation and said that he loved this place. The *Pit*. He said it was like they were in a sci-fi B-movie, where civilization had collapsed and teenagers scavenged the land for food and fuel, and they were the last of the survivors. "Isn't it like that?" he said to James, who agreed. Tag said that there was even quicksand. Just like in the movies. They had quicksand over by the power station.

"Ah," Micah said. "That's just mud."

Kessinger asked if he had seen it, and Micah said that he had not seen it, but that's all that quicksand is, is just mud, and mud dries, so it's probably not there anymore.

"It's always there," Kessinger said, which was true. A few months prior, they had been by the power station, and they had seen a crow that had gotten trapped in the muck. Its wings were painted gray, and if birds at some point in history had decided to begin showing facial expressions, this was the moment. Eventually, the bird had sunk, its black beak rasping into invisibility.

Micah explained that quicksand occurred when the seepage forces oppose the force of gravity and suspend the soil. "That's all it is. It's not that big of a deal. It's all Hollywood and folklore."

"Okay, James," Kessinger said. "I dare you to go in the quicksand. If there's no such thing as quicksand, then you've got nothing to worry about."

"He doesn't have anything to worry about," Micah said.

Stephanie reiterated her position that Kessinger was a douche, and Melinda told him to lay off.

Micah said that Kessinger had a point. They couldn't just walk around claiming this and claiming that, then deciding when and where they were going to back it up. How would they have any credibility? "Let's go," he said.

By the time Tag reached home, the sky had turned the kind of brilliant cobalt that allows the light from only a handful of stars to punch through—orange already beginning to color the horizon. He knew that his parents had not noticed his absence because Clearwater was not presently crawling with police cars flashing beams between houses, choppers flying low, scouring the land with spotlights. From two houses away, Tag could see his father through the kitchen window. From the motion of his arms, he could tell his father was cutting up bananas to put on his cereal, and he made it back through his bedroom without any gaffes that might have given him away. In two hours, his parents would be waking him up for church, and he would be in the middle of the congregation, doodling away on the program foldout, marking off the minutes one at a time, but for the moment, he whiled away his last moments before sleep and meditated on all of the possibilities.

When the teenagers had stood over the muck, Kessinger pointed out that it was not normal quicksand, but the mud was a kind of silt that would not allow for the same margin of error as normal mud. Micah said he knew. He knew about all of this. Silt was a finer grain, muckier than muck, and less forgiving, but particles were particles and water was water, and when combined, they all behave the same way. Kessinger said that Micah was right, except that quicksand is never forgiving. When it is forgiving, then it's not quicksand. Quicksand occurs when the water cannot escape, but if he really believed what he was saying, then why should James be the one to go in? Shouldn't the expert be the one to test that theory?

Stephanie called Kessinger an asshole, and Melinda said they should leave. She held on to James's shirttail, and Kessinger stepped up to Micah, who paused before saying, "Why should James go in?"

For a moment, Tag thought about the music he had made in his bedroom that night with the cassette players—the echo and reverberation. He recalled a third sound. Just as the music began to separate, to fall out of phase, a high-pitched ultrasonic grinding sound appeared as if produced by the air between the boom boxes—the sound of a quiet jet engine whining and descending before dissipating altogether.

"Why *should* James go in?" Micah said.

"Leave it," Stephanie said.

"I'm serious," Micah said. "You believe or you don't," and he slipped off his black dress shoes, removed his shirt and tie, then stepped out of his slacks. Micah stood at the edge of the muck facing the others, held out his arms as if to show that he had nothing to hide, then took a step backward, with an air of confidence and grace. The ground had been built up at the edge of the moat, and Micah looked down upon them with a gaze.

"He'll do it," Stephanie said.

"Why shouldn't I?" Micah said.

Tag understood, however, that Micah was not gazing at them at all, and Micah observed them through neither a lens of love nor pity, only debits and credits.. Micah stepped back, and his right foot disappeared into the muck up to his calf, and his left knee buckled, forcing his body to tumble backward, his body falling back with a slap on the surface followed by the sucking sound of exaggerated digestion. Micah's arms spread out to his side and his entire head plunged into the silt before he arched his back and created enough buoyancy to allow his face to remain above the surface while his fingertips instinctively gripped the quicksand.

The girls screamed, and Kessinger said he was a pussy. Kessinger told Melinda and Stephanie to shut it, and he tossed a shirt sleeve to Micah and told him to grab it, damn it, and keep his back arched. James tried to measure a jump across the muck, then ran alongside the edge and crawled under the fence bordering Union Street, edging along the opposite side of the moat.

"Just take it," Kessinger said again to Micah, then tossed James the pair of pants and told him to try and reach him from there. "Keep your arms out, you dumb shit. Keep your back straight. Get your ass up," he said. "Just sit tight."

Micah's eyes opened and shut like flaps. His face was smeared with wet silt reflecting silver in the onset of morning. "Hey," Kessinger elbowed Tag. "Look at his mouth," he said, pointing out Micah's face, his lips closing tight, then opening wide and gasping for oxygen. "He's almost like a fish."

"Get him," Tag said.

"We'll get him," Kessinger said, bending down at the edge, pulling the pants back in, then flinging them out again within Micah's reach. "Grab it, big boy," he said to Micah. "Come on. Remember, it isn't even quicksand."

BLUEPRINT

The edges of Kessler's road rash seemed almost intentional. The asphalt on Shades Crest Road had scraped deep into the back of his thigh, down to the meat, with striations and tiny black grains of clot dotting the flesh. The laceration, however, appeared buffered around the edges, as if part of his leg had been grated and tenderized, then a specialist had been called in to score the perimeter with a wire brush, making sure that the textures blended an even transition from wound to skin. He showed us a patch on his head, too, like a little wad of bear meat behind his ear. Kessler's hair grew so thick and dense, finding the wound in his scalp took some groping. He worked open a section with his fingertips, showing us the quarter-sized gash, still bright red. He said he didn't even know it was there until he got home from the emergency room. He had been wearing a helmet, but he assumed he had blacked out during the wreck.

Kessler said that he had been riding his moped on Shades Crest Road and had tried to pass a car, only to discover that the car he was passing, along with the asshole in the oncoming vehicle, had taken offense and pressed him. "I gunned it," Kessler said, "but just as I slipped between them, the bumper of the car behind me clipped my back wheel. Half of my ass is still on the side of the road."

"Jesus," Fisher said.

"I gotta rub a salve on this shit twice a day," Kessler said. "They got a salve on it right now to keep it from sticking to the bandage." Kessler opened the tape and held open the bandaging.

"Look, but don't touch it."

"Like hell I'm going to touch it," Fisher said.

I told him it looked like there were still bits of gravel in the meat, but Kessler said it was just clots. A deep, honey-colored goo had soaked into the inside of the dressing.

"The fuckers didn't even stick around," he said. "They knocked me off on purpose."

"That's attempted murder. You should have called the cops," Fisher said.

"My leg was in strips," Kessler said, resealing the surgical tape and pulling up his pajama bottoms.

"What about the moped?" I said. "Can you still ride the moped?"

"Finished. Besides, they got me on dope," Kessler ran his thumb along the tape for a tight seal. "I couldn't stay upright if I wanted to."

It was after eleven o'clock at night. I was staying overnight at Fisher's house, and when his mom had gone to sleep, he and I had slipped out of his kitchen door and headed off towards Kessler's house in the Shady Acres subdivision. We had stashed a bag of toilet paper in the woods, and our plan was for the three of us to climb on Kessler's moped and hit a battery of houses on O'Neal Drive. Sixteen rolls of Scott Tissue. The houses we had in mind begged for toilet paper. A cherry tree on the north side of the lawn with a sweetgum tree on the opposite end, with a smallish Japanese maple next to the brick porch. Another yard formed a canopy of pine trees, tall, with the pine needles bunched at the ends of the branches, with plenty of space to hurl the roll up inside without too much interference. While many of our classmates rolled each others' houses, creating internal feuds and rivalries, in my mind, that approach offered a low-level payoff. For me, it was all about aesthetics, capturing a single element of beauty, masked as vandalism. That was it. Once a proper landscape spoke to me, I had to have it. After that, mapping out the logistics and escape routes and accumulating rolls became a simple matter and almost pleasant task, refreshing my burgeoning teenage angst. Even better, I also lived on O'Neal Drive, and my parents would assume I was nowhere in the vicinity.

Kessler coughed as he locked his bedroom door, lowered himself to the floor and reached deep between his mattress and box spring. He removed a baggie, then held up his hand for assistance back to his feet. "Don't worry, ladies," he said. "We still have plans. Check it out." Kessler handed the baggie to me, with a two-inch one-hitter inside and a quarter inch of dried herb. The mouthpiece had a little ring-shaped nub, and the end had blackened with char and resin. I handed the baggie to Fisher.

"No buds," Fisher said.

"No *buds*," Kessler said. "What do you know about buds?"

"It's all shake," Fisher said. Whenever Fisher spoke, tiny balls of saliva formed in the corners of his mouth, and when he spoke, spit strings stretched from his tongue to the roof of his mouth. All the time, no matter what. It was a disgusting thing to watch.

"Buds are a myth," Kessler said. "The rest of this is good enough on its own. You don't even want buds with this stuff. You get buds with this stuff and you may never come back." He cleaned the end of the pipe with a safety pin and packed it with weed. "Besides," Kessler said, "even if my moped wasn't in pieces, we couldn't go out tonight, anyway. My parents are still up. They're in an uproar. Mr. Lavender, our blessed homeroom teacher, is getting fired. Haven't you assholes heard?"

I told Kessler I hadn't heard anything. Neither had Fisher.

"All the parents are talking about it. They made a petition. Some of the parents even went to his house and delivered it in person."

"He lives in Hoover," Fisher said.

"So what?" Kessler said.

I knew where Mr. Lavender and his wife lived. Mrs. Lavender taught at our school, too, and their kids were a few years below us. They lived at the bottom of Patton Chapel Road near Simmons Junior High. Our soccer team had gone to his house one night at the end of our season. We had started the evening with a hayride, our coach driving us around Shades Mountain while we wrestled in the hay, tossing bale after bale at cars driving behind us. We ended the evening at Mr. Lavender's house, where he hosted a party. We roasted hot dogs and marshmallows in his backyard, Patton Creek running just beyond the border of their property. Of course, the willow tree in his front yard made an impression on me, a large inverted bowl of vines—a tough tree to handle, but not without its potential.

"That's right, my friends," Kessler said. "A bunch of parents went down to his house and knocked on his door."

"When?" I said.

"*Today*. After school. Where have you jerks been?"

We had been at Fisher's house. Fisher's mother was not as tuned in as other parents. Fisher only stayed with her on the weekends, and during the week he slept at his grandparents' house on Savoy. His dad had left the scene when he was five, and Fisher's mom had him when she was only fifteen. Fisher's mom was only twenty-seven, and by all of our classmates' calculations, we all had a legitimate shot. Fisher's mom was a subject of constant fascination. She attended none of the school functions, and when you spent the night at Fisher's house, you ate pizza for dinner and banana pancakes for breakfast. There was also her donning a Mickey Mouse night shirt that left her bare legs exposed all the way up to there. Pure leg. Biblical stuff. At night she was in her room by eight-thirty and the blue light emanating from her television turned to black by eleven, which allowed Fisher and me to ease out the kitchen door and into the neighborhoods.

"Well, my friends," Kessler said. "'Tis true. Mr. Lavender is finished. Done for. My folks have been bitching about him all day. Teaching evolution. They're bitching about him now in the playroom. They'll be bitching about him tomorrow. They'll be bitching about him for years. So will your parents."

"My mom won't," Fisher said. "She believes in evolution."

"Man, if I could get in the pants of just one mother, it'd be yours, my friend," Kessler said. "Every single thing."

Mr. Lavender, our seventh-grade homeroom and math teacher, had opened the morning devotion with a passage from Leviticus. Mr. Lavender had a habit of wearing polyester leisure suits, and he read the morning Bible verses, holding the Bible in front of his face, sitting half-cheeked on his desk in the center of the classroom, an American flag on one side, the Christian flag on the other, extending his index finger as if we should focus our eyes on this single point, then reading aloud, emphasizing a slow random pattern of words. "And if a man lie with a beast," Mr. Lavender read, "he shall surely be put to death: and ye shall slay the beast. And if a woman approach unto any beast, and lie down thereto, thou shalt kill the woman, and the beast: they shall surely be put to death; their blood shall be upon them."

The big question from some of the girls in the class was, why slay the beast? They demanded an answer. Soon, theories abounded. Another friend of ours, Finch, claimed that every sperm cell in the semen constituted a potential human life. Therefore, if the sperm cells worked their way into the bloodstream and into the muscle tissue of the donkey, or the goat, or goose, or what have you, then technically, eating the meat would be an act of cannibalism, of sorts. In that case, the individual eating the meat would have to be put to death, too. Better to just slay the beast and be done with it.

Mr. Lavender then told the class that it was important to consider the timing of the passage. Timing was everything in the Bible, he said. Mr. Lavender said that the Old Testament existed during a time when humankind was not fully evolved. He said that in the time of Moses, humans were *almost* evolved, but they were just a fraction of a chromosomal twist from becoming fully active and genetically complete human beings. With this in mind, Mr. Lavender explained that you had to understand that in some cases, in the Old Testament, the DNA of humans could still mix and match with animals, and while some ancient pervert might think his or her own actions was their own business— that same ancient pervert could inadvertently create an entirely new species. Therefore, not just the individual engaging in this abomination must be slayed, but the animal, too. Pronto.

Kessler held the one-hitter to his lips and drew, turning the tip orange, the flame bending around the circumference. He passed it to Fisher, who pulled and handed it to me. The flame turned a right angle and shot straight into the tube, superheating the smoke and burned the back of my throat. Kessler repacked the pipe and we passed it around for a second lap, again the flame turning ninety-degrees and scorching. After a third lap, Kessler took a can of air freshener out of his underwear drawer and fogged the room, the chemical fumes turning my lungs into glass.

"Okay, boys," Kessler said. "I have something important to tell you."

"Lay it on us," Fisher said.

"Mr. Lavender was right about the DNA. Not many people realize this, but it's true. The guy's a prick, and I'm glad he's out of here, and I could give a shit less if his kids have to the leave the school, or if his wife gets fired, too. I don't give a hang about that, but he's right. However, it goes deeper. Not many people realize this, but in fact, not everyone in the Old Testament fully evolved into humans. Why do you think God was smiting so many people in the Old Testament? The Midianites. Jeroboam. He turned Lot's wife into stone. Why?"

"Why not?"

"Because they weren't people. You get rid of them just like you get rid of an infestation. They are faulty breeds. Think about it. The Israelites weren't the chosen people, they were the *only* people. Not until the time of Christ did the rest of the humans catch up with evolution, except that some of those strains of almost-humans were so close to the human race that they continued to breed. They continue to breed, to this day, and it is impossible to tell who is and who isn't one of these almost humans. They're all around us. They fill up jails, they teach schools, run banks and businesses. They run the government. In fact, many people in positions of power are these non-humans, because they are compensating subconsciously for that essential element they lack. They walk among us. And since they're not real people, they have no access to spiritual blessings or salvation. These beings are undetectable. I mean, tell me something. Do either of you know the difference between a donkey and a mule?"

"I do," Fisher said.

"The fuck you do," Kessler said, bringing the pipe to his lips, then pulling it away. "When these beings die, they go to neither Heaven nor Hell. They just decay like animals or bugs, or whatever."

Kessler turned the tip of the pipe orange again, then passed it. He held his breath while we looked, and then he exhaled and spoke again. "Sociopaths are like this. They kill indiscriminately because they don't see any reason not to. Ted Bundy was probably one of these. Those assholes who tried to run me over were probably these non-humans."

I wished Kessler would change the subject, and I regretted smoking the dope in the first place. After all, my heart was outside in the darkness, slinging Scott Tissue high into sweetgums, weaving a white web in the branches, the tissue paper streaming back to the ground like a perfect brush stroke, all muscle memory and divine guidance, transforming the yard into some kind of space age anemone, a living, breathing organism. Cool white tendrils against an ink-dark sky.

"Now I'm going to tell you something you're not going to like," Kessler said.

"I already don't like it," Fisher said.

"I have bad news," Kessler said. "Good news and bad news."

"Christ," Fisher said.

"Tonight, one of us will gain the realization that we are one of these breeds. Tonight, one of us will know he is different."

"Bullshit," Fisher said.

"I don't know which of us it is going to be, but I have actually studied this stuff, so I have a sense for it."

Almost immediately, I felt the urge to bark.

"The good news is that one of us will no longer have to worry about Heaven or Hell. Scratch that off the table, because that person is worm food. In other words, one of us has no soul."

"How do you know it isn't you?" Fisher said.

"I *don't* know," Kessler said.

"You act like it isn't you," Fisher said.

"Hell, it might *be* me," Kessler said. "It might be either of you. And if it is one of us, then it will be your offspring, too, so consider that."

From my point of view, I knew it wasn't Fisher's mom. No way was she part animal, not with that macrodont smile and unblemished thighs. But of course, Fisher's dad could have passed him the defective gene. No doubt. It very easily could have been Fisher, with those gaps in his teeth and the spit strings, his head bobbing and floating above his shoulders like it was never going to fit. Maybe that was why his dad had split. Maybe his dad just humped his mom, then found some other leg to climb.

Kessler held up his hand and listened for his parents' voices.

"Mr. Lavender did not get fired," Fisher said in a whisper.

"Hey," Kessler said. "I didn't say I liked this information," Kessler said. "I didn't say I wanted it to happen, but it is the way it is, and there's nothing we can do about it. Just because you do not want your world to change doesn't mean it isn't going to change. Tonight, one of us will know he is different."

I started to talk, but as soon as my vocal chords started to vibrate, a feeling of mystery swept over me as if I had no idea if the sound emitted from my mouth would be intelligible words or my own voice barking. I could feel it sitting there in the back of my throat waiting to jump out. Thank *God* there were no buds, I thought. I could hear with my skin. I could feel time, silver blue and metallic transparent, reflective on the surface, but clear if you looked close enough. The stuff dripped from my fingertips. The stuff seethed through my hair and into my follicles, and now my voice. The last thing I wanted to think about was genetic malfunctions.

"Shit," Kessler said. "My parents." In the matter of a thought, Fisher and I were out the window, jumping to the pitch-black shadow of a loblolly pine, landing awkwardly in a bed of straw, then bounding up and taking off past the Baptist church towards Fisher's house.

The urge to bark remained. It sat there in the back of my throat, so much so that I was afraid to say anything lest it jump out, but it was there already. Like a pill stuck in your throat that had somehow come to life, just waiting to erupt and give yourself away.

* * *

I was in no shape to go back to Fisher's house. I could see myself waking up in the pre-dawn hours howling and whining, scratching at the inside of Fisher's bedroom door, bugged out with border frustration. I would wake up the entire house. Fisher, his brother, his mom. She would call my folks. They would drive me down to see our family doctor, get me hopped up on brain anchors and anti-anxiety pills. They would put me in Special Ed., and my classmates would smell like Doritos and wear teenage diapers. They would call the News. Fisher was in no shape, either. No sooner had we made it into the street did he pull a butterfly knife from his sock and start whipping it open and closed like some kind of tic, clicking and clacking, glistening sharpened metal under lamplight.

Fisher and I walked down to the edge of Shady Acres, grabbed our stash of Scott Tissue and cut through the Woodland subdivision with a change of plans. The houses on O'Neal were out, and within minutes it seemed, we were strolling down Patton Chapel Road headed for Hoover—the whole time, my thirst for ululation bulging in the back of my throat. I couldn't even open my mouth, lest this new thing erupt and turn everything inside out. Who knows, maybe I would charge down the asphalt, chasing motorcycles and passing cars, yammering away with bared fangs? Christ. If anything, it was Kessler who was part animal. If you thought about it, Kessler had the hair of goat or some kind of seal gene. I had never even seen his hair wet, it was so thick. Anytime he stepped out of the pool or the shower, all it took was a quick shake and he was dry. And Fisher with his spit strings. No way was Fisher all human.

Patton Chapel Road provided a straight shot down to Mr. Lavender's house. Moonlight washed over the asphalt, giving the night and road ahead a dreamlike, peaceful feeling, with the landscape to the left, leaving an orange wall of clay, with blackened rows of erosion ruts. To the right, the landscape sank into undeveloped forest. Headlights shined a mile away each direction, and avoiding detection was as easy as stepping over the guard rail and ducking down until the light passed. You could walk right down the middle of the road with the white stripe of the Milky Way overhead. You could take your time walking straight away, but it felt like the opposite of walking in a dream, where everything is muddy and slow. Walking down Patton Chapel felt like the ground was spinning beneath our feet.

But the weeping willow in Mr. Lavender's house was not as I had remembered at all. My mind had imprinted an image of a reversed bowl, vine-like branches streaming from the top down in perfect symmetry, but the tree before us was taller than his bi-level house, with cascading bulbs of growth, layers of inverted bowls on top of the other. One of our classmates had given an oral report of Japanese poetry accompanied by a painting illustrating the poem, and seeing the weeping willow under moonlight reminded me of that precise image.

"I'm going to slash their tires," Fisher said.

I waved off Fisher and motioned for him to stay put and toss rolls to me when I needed them. *Tire slashing.* Jesus Christ. If I needed any more proof of Fisher's faulty DNA, that was it. Egging houses, keying cars, uprooting stop signs, slashing tires, these types of vandalism were for brutes and the aesthetically retarded. Lower breeds. No sensitivity whatsoever. But the prick disappeared, leaving me to hoist myself up into the tree, wrapping individual limbs, one by one, like placing the skeleton of the tree into a body cast—a burdensome task no doubt, but necessary to achieve the overall effect.

I could envision the final scene, the tree in full dressing—a composition of three voices. The solid white interior, coupled with streams flowing from the branches beneath each bowl. Finally, rather than tossing the rolls from the outside over the top, I would throw them from the inside out, creating individual streams erupting from within. I could only imagine the thrill of seeing the creation first hand, reflecting only the light of nearby streetlamps, and the slow transition from moonlight to morning sun. I wanted to let out just one single howl to get me off and set the mood, but then I saw Fisher's figure bolting through the neighbor's lawn toward Patton Chapel. The little tire slasher was off, the fucker. I could see Fisher breaking through lamplight and into the backyard of the house across the street, disappearing into the darkness. I froze. I could wait it out. I had it in my blood. I read about coon dogs that can sit for days at the base of a tree waiting for their victim to surrender. All I needed to do was remain silent. I could have done it too, but for the pair of white Nikes canvas shoes with the powder-blue stripe, supporting two trunks of the hairiest legs I had ever seen. I had never seen Mr. Lavender out of his polyester leisure suit. He wore close-cropped denim cutoff shorts, and he stood with his knees locked, giving his stance a slightly deformed look, though his thigh muscles bulged, as if all of the tension from his miserable day had gathered in his quads. He stepped into the canopy, pointed up at me with his index finger and directed his finger toward the ground. "Get down," he said, then took me by the back of the shirt up his front porch, through their living room and set me down at his kitchen table.

His wife, Mrs. Lavender, who had also been my fifth-grade teacher, entered the kitchen in her bathrobe without making eye contact with me. She wore green terrycloth socks that left her calves slightly exposed, revealing the driest skin I had ever seen. Chapped, even. She prepared two cups of instant coffee, then returned to the living room with her husband. The clock on their wall above the sink showed that it was only one o'clock in the morning.

Mr. Lavender returned and sat down across the table. Mr. Lavender's eyes bulged in such a way that added a layer of surprise to each of his emotions and expressions. Surprised anger, surprised joy, surprised arrogance and pity, grief and boredom, but the layer of surprise also suggested that you were aware of this element, a physical disconnect that created an immediate distance no matter what emotion the moment required. "I don't suppose your parents sent you," he said. Before I had the chance to answer, he put down his coffee and said, "What's wrong with you people?"

Too afraid to answer with some sort of modified yelp, I shrugged my shoulders.

"All of you," he said. "I saw your parents here, tonight. Your mom and dad." I nodded my head, but Mr. Lavender told me to shut up. "Just shut up," he said. He sipped his coffee and said that of all the people who had come to their house that night, not one person had bothered to knock on his door. Not one of them had bothered to ask for a clarification, or how his wife and children might be affected by the event. Not one. Not a single pair of gonads in the whole goddamned bunch. "And they were my family. They have been my family for the past seven years. I have opened my doors to you people, I have picked your kids up from soccer practice, visited you in the hospital, taught you, guided many of you through tough times, and without knowing the facts of a single morning's devotional, you people show up to my house during dinner with a petition for my resignation, with candles, singing hymns. We have broken bread together." Mr. Lavender sipped his coffee again, then said, "I get a call one hour later from Dr. Federman to let me know that I have been replaced, that I am no longer welcome on campus. The contents of my desk will be boxed and mailed to me. Dr. Federman informs me that Marnie has also been replaced and our kids will not be allowed at school Monday morning. We have now, tomorrow, and Sunday to find new schooling for both of them. No severance package, no housing assistance. All in one day. How do your parents feel about that?"

Mr. Lavender stood and added another spoon of coffee to his cup and topped it off with water from the kettle. Their kettle seemed to be covered with ages of caked oil. The water must have been low, as Mr. Lavender had to turn the kettle almost completely upside down to get any water. For some reason, he muttered, "Goddamned Marnie," then returned to the table. Mrs. Lavender returned, too, and sat next to the window overlooking their backyard. "Don't be shy on me now," Mr. Lavender said. "Were you in the car with your parents tonight?"

I shook my head.

"Don't bullshit me, kid," he said. Mrs. Lavender winced, then looked at me as if both critical and accepting of her husband's use of profanity.

"Honey," Mrs. Lavender said to her husband.

"*Marnie,*" he said, then redirected his attention to me.

Just like that, I could feel the bulge in the back of my throat start to give. I ran my thumb against the fingertips just to make sure they had not transformed throughout the evening. I closed my eyes and could see the color-opposite outlines of Mr. Lavender and wife, along with every detail in their kitchen. I remembered the night he had invited the soccer team over for the cookout, how I had entered their kitchen for water, and all the glasses in their cupboard were the type of textured glassware that looked both solid and shattered at the same time.

Suddenly, I got dizzy. I didn't know why he had yet to call my parents or ask if anybody else was with me, but maybe it was all part of his routine. Calculating what kind of punishment might be doled out to me was beyond any present understanding, but it would be severe and dense. I had not only snuck out, but I had snuck out of a friend's house, a double betrayal of trust. Vandalism. And why wouldn't the police get involved? What then? Did the cops take you in, let you sit at their desk while you waited for your parents, or did they put you behind bars, vulnerable to all of the terror and violence of jail?

Mr. Lavender looked at his wife and took another sip of coffee. The pressure was such that I feared a real possibility of Mr. Lavender standing up and swinging, leaping over the table, one hand on my shirt collar and the other delivering a beatdown, leaving me to figure out a way to survive, with or without Mrs. Lavender pulling him from me. Maybe that was the moment I was looking for, when I knew it wasn't me with the faulty genes. Animals don't wonder how they will survive. They have instincts. Animals crave these moments, even in the throes of a death match. But not me. I sat opposite my two former teachers petrified. In my silence, I felt a wave of relief. Send the cops, send my folks. I'll take it from there.

But Mr. Lavender didn't swing. Instead, he dug in. He took another slug of coffee and started rolling, talking about Moses coming down the mountain barking orders at the purebreds, prophecies, trajectories and doctrine.

"Let me ask you something," Mr. Lavender said. "Cain murders Abel. Right? That's what it says, doesn't it?"

I shrugged my shoulders.

"Well, did he?"

I nodded my head.

"That's right. He did. He denies this charge and then his crime is discovered. He is cast out into the wilderness and he is marked, isn't he?"

I nodded.

"Well? Tell me something, my friend. Tell me. After Cain is marked, who are these people out there who are going to take him down? Which individuals roaming out there in the desert are going to see this message?"

I looked at Mrs. Lavender then back at Mr. Lavender.

"Have you ever considered the possibility, the vague, wild chance, that Adam and Eve may not have been the first humans, but simply the first to understand the difference between good and evil, the first to achieve existential thought—the hallmark of the human mind? Have you ever considered that these two figures might have been the first to evolve, both physically and spiritually? Or that they simply represent the collective evolution? Because you still haven't answered me. Who are those out there in the wilderness who will be instructed to avenge Abel's death?" Mr. Lavender sipped his coffee and smiled. He did that in class, too, anytime he established a brief moment in time where the words that uttered from his lips proved that he was smarter than you. He smiled and waited until somebody in the class acknowledged the moment. "Might the people out there in the wilderness be those who have yet to make this distinction?" He looked at Mrs. Lavender, then back at me. "Sounds like a bunch of people I know, doesn't it?"

Mr. Lavender paused, pointed at me with his coffee mug. "The purpose of the spiritual gift is twofold. One purpose if for you to glorify God, and the other purpose is for everyone else. The *macro*. You see, when the Lord has bequeathed upon you your own spiritual gift, you are guided by the gift, and order follows. Policemen enforce the law with divine judgment and benevolence. Musicians play to praise, and they will practice their instrument insufferably until their instrument sings of devotion. But the selfish musician plays for his own physical pleasure. The selfish policeman governs only according to law and his own sense of power. Drug addicts function according to their next fix. Their addiction dictates that they live nearby dealers, leaving addicts to prostitution and violence. Drunkards are given order by drink. Now, my friend. Look around. Our society is guided by darkness. Our entire country is structured by laws, not what heights you shall reach. You follow?"

"No," I said.

"You don't follow."

"I don't know," I said.

"We are guided, collectively, by restriction. It is all of us. You, me, Marnie, your classmates, your *parents*. We know intellectually that we are to find our gift, to find the spirit, but look around. Not one of us is capable of recognizing the Spirit."

Mrs. Lavender, *Marnie*, leaned her hip against the kitchen counter and brought her cup of tea to her mouth with both hands.

"Well, I've got news for you," Mr. Lavender said. "Not even the Chosen are chosen anymore. We're not post-tribulation. We are *post-Millennium*. Simon Peter's vision tells us that the pollution is complete." Mr. Lavender sipped his coffee again. "We're all polluted. We are post-light, post-illumination."

I looked at Mr. and Mrs. Lavender, and I could hear a sound in the driveway beneath the kitchen window. The sound of snapping rubber, and the white spray of compression. One, then another. My heart sprang. Even the click-clacking of the butterfly knife between punctures. At the same time, my heart sank, too. The Lavenders first jumped to the kitchen window, then sprang to the kitchen door leading to the driveway. I found myself standing, watching them fight through the glare to identify the sounds from outside, and my feet kept on into the living room, where all it took was a sudden move to the front door and I was out, down the steps of their porch, in the yard, weightless, with a clear vision of a pathway through the shadows. I ran without hesitation until I was in the clear, sprinting up the moonlit pavement on Patton Chapel Road, fearless of the headlights I could spot coming all the way down the road. Once I reached a safe distance, out of shouting range, however, I gave in to temptation and let out a series of howls. First an extended wail, starting low, quickly raising the pitch, as if casting the sound vibrations directly over the hills into Shades Crest, so loud I could hear the echo, then rifled off a burst of rapid-fire yips, until finishing off with a deep bellow, a lungful generated from the diaphragm, enough reach and volume to mix timbres with the slapback, then resumed walking towards Bluff Park. I would be back in the sack in no time. Easy. Hours before sunup. Hours before Fisher's mother would cook up a batch of banana pancakes.

STRIPPING ROSES

The job paid five dollars an hour, but it paid cash, and Mrs. West promised future employment at West Farms Florist if things stayed busy after Valentine's Day. Mrs. West had a Southern bouffant that I didn't trust, but the next morning I met her husband at their shop on Archer Road, and he drove me and a guy named Bankowski to the farm way out past I-75 into horse country. Mr. West picked us up at six-thirty, and the morning Florida fog seethed in and out of the Spanish moss and live oaks all the way down Archer Road to the farm. Mr. West took us to the shed where we met Harold, his cousin, who was going to be stripping roses with us. If the wind blew right, you could get a steady waft of horse manure. They kept the roses bundled up in boxes where they had been shipped from Peru. Mr. West told us they had to order extra roses, because they rammed steel blades into the sheaves at Customs to make sure they aren't loaded with cocaine. Predicting how many roses would be destroyed was impossible.

Mr. West told us to strip the five boxes here. When we were done with these boxes, separate them into long, medium and short stems. Take out the longest stems and put them in a stack. The long stems need the thorns intact. Once we had a stack; tie them into dozens. Then he pointed to the barn where the boxes had been stacked in three columns ten boxes high. On average, he told us, stripping twenty-thousand roses required three ten-hour days, so it came out to fifty per day. If we finished early, it was fifty. If we finished late, it was fifty.

Mr. West handed us each a metal tool to strip the thorns. He demonstrated, fitting the mouth of the gadget around the stem, then pulled down in a swift tug, shooting thorns out the sides. Thorns nicked your hands no matter how you held it, so Mr. West told us that we had better use our gloves. I had forgotten to bring any gloves, and he told me that I should have brought them. I asked if they had some in the barn, but Mr. West told me that it would be better to use mine. I asked him if we could check, and he said that I should have brought my own gloves. Harold told me that if I rubbed my palms at the end of the day with garlic juice and Vitamin E they'd be good as new in the morning, which I tried when I got home that evening, but he failed to report that the sting of garlic shoots down where the nerves meet the joints and makes silver and purple lights light up behind your eyelids.

The three of us drank coffees and listened to the morning news, and broadcasters announced that the trade embargo against Iraq had caused perhaps more damage to archeological sites than the war itself. Harold said *boo-hoo*. Assholes like Saddam Hussein rape their own women, gas their own people, *spy* on their own people, and then people get bent out of shape because of archeological sites. Boo-*damn*-hoo. "Give me freedom, or give me archeology. I'll take freedom," he said.

We listened to music until lunch. Mrs. West fixed us tuna sandwiches that had a funny taste, but they worked. I took a stroll to work the stiffness out of my legs. I thought about bolting and even walked a half-mile towards Bronson to see if maybe they didn't have a bus, but decided against it. On the walk back, I counted over two hundred-fifty tiny cuts on the palms of each hand. When I returned, somebody had put it back to the news channel.

"Hey there, latecomer," Harold said.

"How long have you two been back at work?" I said.

"Long enough," Bankowski said.

"Listen," Harold said, nodding at the radio.

I placed the gadget around a stem and jerked. The broadcaster repeated the announcement. The report was in from the Alachua County Police Department. They had made an arrest. Neighbors had called complaining of violence next door, and a young man had beaten up his grandmother. During the arrest, an altercation had ensued. The man was twenty-two years of age, and his face had been badly scarred, and witnesses claimed that he was wild-eyed. After some speculation, the police determined that the young man in question was the prime suspect for the killings. They had him. The fear that had gripped central Florida was over. "It is a good day for daughters. It is a good day for parents. It is good day for all of us," the radio said. The radio announced that the moratorium on walking alone was off, and young people could once again frequent Lake Allison after dark, but still, lock your doors and use your best judgment, but the relief, the broadcaster said, was palpable. The newscaster recounted the entire scene of the murders and repeated all the details, with which we were all familiar. The radio man revisited the crowbar and gore, the couple locking themselves inside to wait for help that never came, the mirrors, the arrangements, all designed for amplified terror.

"Gas him," Harold said.

"Gas him nothing," Bankowski said. "He needs to feel more than gas."

Harold said it was times like this that they needed to suspend due process. Look at those girls he had cut up. Did we know what he had done to those girls? Harold said he had not seen the pictures, but he did not want to see the pictures; what he had read was enough.

"Did you hear what he did with the scalps?" Bankowski said.

"Don't talk about it," Harold said.

"You don't want to know," Bankowski said.

"I think I can use my imagination," I said.

"I don't want to use my imagination for that shit," Harold said. "Unless you're some kind of sicko. Leave me out of it." Harold said that the killer had rearranged the girls after, and anybody who used their imagination for that was probably just as guilty. Harold said the monster they had picked up, had put them in positions, and *monster* wasn't really the word.

Harold dumped the empty cardboard and Bankowski fetched a couple more from the barn. We ripped open a new box of roses, and you couldn't help but do the math as you stripped and bundled. I didn't want to think about how much we were earning per rose, but after a time, you can't help but start calculating. Twenty thousand divided by twelve. Five times ten times three. Sixteen hundred divided by four-fifty. I kept getting my figures mixed up, but there was plenty of time to mix and match the numbers, and I didn't even want to think about it. They put the music station back on, then after a time it seemed like somebody was always ripping open another box and taking one down from the barn.

I liked bundling the long stems. I told Harold I wouldn't mind sticking around. I could do this kind of work all the time. I told him what Mrs. West had said something about taking me on permanently, but he didn't answer. I could see myself doing that kind of work. Snip the stems, keep the water fresh, wrap the bundles in Mylar, tell people they made a beautiful selection. How hard could it be? Harold seemed preoccupied, and I could tell he was thinking about the killer. I was right. He zipped a stem of thorns then said he wasn't sure what kind of asshole lawyer would go around defending somebody who either beats up his grandmother or cuts people up. "How do people stand in front of a judge and jury and look them in the eye and say that they should just walk free?" Harold said that due process was not established for people like that. Laws were made for normal people. They had him, they knew it was him, and they didn't need to waste anymore of taxpayers' money on him. They had wasted enough. Take him out back, that's it.

"I don't know," I said. "I don't know about that guy."

"What don't you know?" Bankowski said.

"I don't think he did it."

"Oh, no?" Harold said. "This guy that beats up his own grandmother? He sounds like a real prince. I tell you what. My heart is not exactly bleeding for this creep."

"Just because he beat up his grandmother?" I said.

Harold gave me a look and asked what kind of asshole beats up his grandmother. Bankowski raised his eyes at me. "Did you listen to the radio?" Harold said.

"I know," I said. "I never said it was good to beat up your grandmother. By general rule, one should never 'beat up their grandmother.' However, my greater point is that nobody beats up their grandmother without provocation, unless the grandmother has touched some nerve."

"Christ," Harold said. "This guy."

We kept stripping roses and bundling, and after a while Bankowski changed the radio to a Top Forty station. They played Richard Marx, the Bangles, Amy Grant, and then broke for a millennium of commercials. Then they returned from the break to play more Richard Marx. I tried to crawl into a deep space in my mind and pretend the music wasn't happening, but sometimes one is powerless. I told the two that if they played one more Richard Marx song the police were going to have to come and pick *me* up for questioning.

On Thursday, after three shifts from morning until mid-afternoon, Mr. West dropped me and Bankowski off at the shop on Archer. I counted the money on the bike ride home and was happy that they had not charged me for the sandwiches Mrs. West had made for us each day. I tucked fifty dollars away for the electricity and water, and when my roommate, Charles Russell, came home, we grocery-shopped. I bought a twenty-pound sack of potatoes, two dozen eggs, a ten-pound bag of apples, two pounds of black beans, three pounds of pintos, a tub of fat from the butcher, a gallon of whole milk, a quart of buttermilk, a quart of goat milk, and some onions. That night we ordered two large pizzas and split a twelve-pack.

Charles Russell sat on his barstool eating pizza from the countertop, and I sat on the beanbag in the middle of our empty living room, facing the sliding glass doors that looked out on the woods. I could see Charles Russell's reflection behind me. I could see him bobbing his head to the music, holding a slice with one hand and raising his other hand a foot from the wall, opening his palm and slamming it against the wall—punishment he doled out to our neighbor for constantly complaining about noise from our apartment.

Moments later, when the phone rang, I watched Charles Russell pick it up and talk to our neighbor. He said he had not heard anything at all. He talked further, and then brought the phone to me. I told Selene, our neighbor, that I had not heard thumps or any sounds, either, but I would be happy to be on the lookout. I agreed, I said, that it was strange.

I told Charles Russell that he had better stop doing stuff like that or people would start calling the cops, and they would have a new murder suspect.

Charles Russell responded by giving the wall another thump. We waited, but Selene must have been too tired to call.

"I'll tell you what," I said. "If that was me out there. If I was the killer, I would take this opportunity to go south. Or north. Or any direction. I would walk right down to the bus station and buy a ticket for the Keys, or Miami, or Okeechobee or something like that. I would not stick around for a heartbeat."

"They got him already," Charles Russell said.

"That's not him," I said. "They're just trying to cool off the hysteria. A killer does not beat up his grandmother. Killers get lazy, or reckless, or careless, but they don't go around beating up grandmothers."

"We'll see," he said. "We shall see."

"If that was me, I would go anywhere but here. Nobody's looking for him now. Nobody's thinking about anything. I would go anywhere else and let them think they had their man. By the time they realized their mistake, I'd be gone."

"Keep talking like that, people are going to think *you're* the killer. I'm serious," he said.

"Think about it," I said. "That guy is out. I mean, he is *out*. And he's probably been out his whole life. Who's going to talk to him? Who's going to sleep with him? He sees a car full of frat boys and sorority girls, and they couldn't care less if he burst into flames. To them, he's walking excrement, much less an object of affection. He's out. He's dirt, and he'll never be allowed in. Just think for a minute what it must be like, the rage you would feel. Think about it. To be sealed away from society, forever."

"I'd keep my clam shut if I were you." Charles Russell took another bite of pizza, then said, "It probably *is* you. You take walks in the woods. You take odd jobs. You do shit like shuck roses. You're like a day laborer. You do drifter work."

We sat for a few more minutes, and then Charles Russell went upstairs for bong hits, and I stayed downstairs for a few more beers, and then I went in the kitchen and ground up a garlic clove and rubbed the juice into my palms. It was worse the first night when I wasn't expecting it. The juice touched the openings and turned into instant fire—white light, white heat, blue flash, then sustaining, then holding, then giving, finally cooling into red, the pain subsiding and coasting into pleasure. Sweet pleasure.

HYPOTHERMIA

The *hog and jog*. The *bolt and jolt*. There's nothing like it. You can try all you want, but there is nothing that tightens the nerves in your abdomen like skipping out on the bill and watching the busboys and dishdogs fill your peripheral vision as you burst through the double glass doors.

This is our goodbye dinner for Alex. He orders a double cheeseburger because he's beefing up for basic training. He's about to leave for the first Gulf War. When Alex got word that Saddam was the new Hitler, he'd ridden his bike down to the recruiter adjacent to the Skyline Chili before you could say hydrogen cyanide. Jessica, Alex's girlfriend, orders a Caesar salad because she's on a perpetual diet. Vanessa, my date, orders buffalo wings, two eggs, a waffle, fruit yogurt and a hamburger with fries, because she's bulimic. She gets the hamburger instead of a cheeseburger because she's Jewish, and she can't mix cow meat with cow milk. I note the yogurt on her order, and she says that she's not *that* Jewish. Just Jewish. I order pancakes and a double order of bacon because I enjoy eating breakfast food for dinner.

When Alex had joined the service, we assumed it was high jinks, a lark, but then he had his physical, and then he signed his papers. If he fails to show up in the morning, he will be considered AWOL. I know part of Jessica's plan is that we'll get busted, and he won't have to go to the Army, and since I'm a little bit in love with Jessica, my plan is that he be there at eight o'clock on the button.

The waitress asks if we want anything to drink. Do they serve beer? They do not. Alex and I get a pot of coffee, Vanessa gets a Coke, and Jessica orders a Tab. Our waitress is a tall, ostrich-legged redhead. You can tell that Big Red experienced about a nano-second flash of beauty in her twenties, a flash that she squandered swilling plastic-bottle vodka in a Clearwater Beach singles bar, now cursed to serve smart-assed teenagers at three a.m. for the next thirty years. But the woman must have some kind of Jedi voodoo, because she knows we're going to skip out on the bill. It's my fault, I know. At this point, I stare at her eyeball to eyeball, trying to convey telepathic messages that all is cool, all is kosher. I try to convey the message that there are a whole slew of universes going on simultaneously. I've been on a serious multi-verse obsession, and I have been trying to tell her that there is one universe where we pay, one where we're the waiters, and one where we bolt. This happens to be the one where we bolt. Therefore, all is cool. All is dandy. All is kosher. We are going to eat, continue eating, find our seam, cruise through the double glass doors and disappear into the darkness. So no need to fret, I tell her with my eyes. I try to assure the waitress that in a very near dimension, we are doubling the tip.

However, all is *not* kosher. When we started the evening at Alex's for a couple cans of beer, we were hitting his fluorescent blue PVC ice bong, chugging down some kind of wicked, throat-scalding skunkweed. We were also watching CNN and the little Kuwaiti princess bleat about the Iraqi soldiers and the incubator babies. The four of us watched in amazement as the girl described the atrocities of Saddam's army. Then, Jessica cut the cannabis haze like a laser-guided Tomahawk missile when she said that the whole thing was a load of crap. She declared that the girl was a tasty little cunt, and you couldn't write a better load of dog shit in Hollywood. I said, "Well," but all of my instincts told me to agree with Jessica. I could tell her comments rubbed Alex the wrong way. She was his girlfriend, and he was less than twenty-four hours from joining the fight. After we poured the bongwater into four evenly divided cups and shot it down, Alex said, pointing to the television, "That's why I signed up. Some jerk-off dictator out there orders his men to burn everything, rape all the women, slaughter the babies, and then his men go out and follow his orders. You know what that tells me?" We waited for an answer, even though we knew the answer. The news on TV had told us told us already, so we knew what was coming. "It tells me that they're not human. They're *in*human."

This is my second date with Vanessa, and nothing like a hog and jog to ward off the sophomore jinx. She and I work together at the Salad Station five miles up U.S. 19—one of those all-you-can-eat places that hypnotize neo-hippie health freaks. I can tell that Jessica neither likes nor approves of Vanessa, which I chalk up to natural female seed-competition. Jessica did not approve of Vanessa from the beginning, though Vanessa barely passed my test as well. But her reputation suggested that my chances were good, and sitting on my shoulders spoke both an angel and public health official, each of them pleading their cases.

On the drive out to Denny's, the conversation about the bleating Kuwaiti girl took a lull, but after Big Red serves our meals, Jessica can't help herself and says, "Babies don't just shrivel up and die when you take them out of incubators. They would eventually die of starvation, or their blood sugar levels would drop, and they would go into shock. They don't just die if you take them out of incubators."

"They would die of hyperthermia," Alex said.

I correct Alex and tell him that if the babies died of

hyperthermia, it would mean that once taken out of the incubators, they would overheat to the point of baking. Their blood would boil, and they would die.

"*Hypothermia*," Jessica says.

"Whatever," Alex says. "They would die. They would die of hypothermia."

"Eventually," Jessica says, "but the girl said that the Iraqi soldiers took them out and watched them die on the cold floor."

"The *cold* floor," Alex says.

"But babies don't just die that easily," Jessica says. "Babies are resilient."

"She was talking about preemies," Alex says. "*Preemies.*"

"Babies have even survived abortions," Jessica says.

I give Jessica a quick look and give her the kill sign, slashing my hand across my throat, nodding my head towards Vanessa.

"I'm just saying that the babies would not die that fast. It takes a while for babies to die. And if these Iraqi soldiers are so savage, they would have just skewered the babies," Jessica says.

"She's right," I say.

"I *am* right," Jessica says, as Big Red comes along with our coffees and sodas. She asks us if we need anything else, and Alex orders a side order of fries and maybe a Reuben, Vanessa gets another waffle and fries, Jessica breaks down and gets a burger, and I get one, too. Then we ask for chocolate shakes all around. Big Red gives us another evil eye, and I reciprocate with my telepathy.

"If these Iraqi soldiers are in the process of invading a country," I say, "and they are as vicious as this Kuwaiti princess claims, would they really waste their time waiting for the slow process of babies succumbing to exposure, what with all of the raping and pillaging to do?" I tell the table that, just as a bystander, if I was a savage Iraqi soldier, I'd make time with that Kuwaiti princess.

"She's *fifteen*," Alex says.

"You're disgusting," Jessica says. "I know what you're trying to say," she dips one of Alex's fries in ketchup, "but you're still kind of disgusting."

"You people are blind," Alex says. "It's sad. That's the problem. It's sad."

"It just smells too weird," Jessica says, continuing to eat Alex's fries. Then Vanessa takes one of his fries, too, dipping it in a monkey dish of mayo, bites only the part of the fry coated in sauce, then dips again and again.

As the second date, it is also the second occasion in over two years that I have not served as the third wheel. Usually, Alex, Jessica and I do everything together. We play miniature golf together. We pack back-packs full of Milwaukee's Best and ride our bikes to Dunedin Causeway and swim across shark-infested inlets to Caledesi Island, or we go way out on Clearwater Beach or Honeymoon Island where there is nobody. We slug beers, then Alex and Jessica crawl off beyond the dunes and sawgrass to hump, while I smoke cigarettes and take a swim out to the dark waters and try to attract hammerheads.

I know why Alex and Jessica keep me around. As Alex's best friend, I'm also their court jester. My skills as permanently lonesome are crafted to keep those around me entertained. I've been able to buy beer since I was seventeen (also Jedi voodoo), juggle fire, funnel beer standing on my head, and lately, there is my obsession with parallel and multiple universes. I'm also the opposite of Alex. Alex's parents pay his rent, buy his car, give him money, a stereo system—everything. And he gets Jessica. I'm Johnny Two-Dollars, even with a job—all of my cash going to repair my '66 Falcon, or tuition for the fall semester at the junior college, or gas, or anything. It's even odd for me to be out with a woman. Where Alex and Jessica touch arms and hands and legs with ease, naturally eat from each other's plates, I can feel each negative ion pulsating between Vanessa and myself. Jessica told me I would be fine, just hang out—be cool—don't be weird. Each time I start to talk about the multi-verse, she holds up her hand and backs me down.

"Just nuke 'em," Vanessa says. "Just drop a bomb on those assholes and be done with the whole fucking war in a day."

"We're not going to start a nuclear war," Alex says. "We may drop a neutron bomb if we absolutely have to, but those bombs are barely bigger than some of the major conventional weapons—and we wouldn't drop them on residential areas, like Saddam does. Trust me on that one. We're going to dismantle the place piece by piece and shove their SCUDs up enough asses until they get the hell out of Kuwait. Kuwait's freedom is our freedom. That's what I'm fighting for."

"That little Kuwaiti princess is a muppet," Jessica says. "Anybody can see that."

"We're all muppets, if you think about it," I say, though I'm not sure exactly what I mean.

"You're a traitor, baby," Alex says to Jessica. "I love you, honey, but they should put you to death." Alex takes a bite of his sandwich that is clearly overestimated, and it is quickly apparent that he isn't finished talking, but he may or may not be able to work the food down his throat, and for a moment, the three of us watch in anticipation. When he accomplishes this peristaltic feat and washes it down with a slug of coffee, he hammers his chest with the side of his fist and says to Jessica, "So you're calling that little girl a liar. That little Kuwaiti girl."

I raise my cup of coffee say, "Well. Here's to Alex giving his life, so we can all be muppets."

"And here's to fighting for our freedom, so you pussies can hog and jog," Alex says.

"And here's to making sweet love to Jessica for the next two years," which very nearly turns out to be true. In the fall, when college starts, Jessica and I move in together in a little shithole off Douglas, in Dunedin, where we share one queen bed between us, no couch, one set of dishes and a single radio for entertainment. For one semester, we live like a team and harmonize. It's her job to wash the dishes and my job to kill the cockroaches living behind the walls and inside the dishwasher. We both attend junior college. She waits tables, and I get a job dogging dishes at Jessie's Dockside, working with ex-cons and assholes and heavy-metal tattoo fiends—and those are the cooks and runners. I'm on the bottom rung sweating it out in the dishpit. Jessica and I both correspond with Alex. She writes him her letters, and I research his war for him, sending him documentation of Kuwait's lateral drilling into Iraq oil fields, a little thank-you gift for protecting them against the wrath of Iran. I tell him that Kuwait is nice enough to hire Iraqi girls as prostitutes, so their sheiks can do their own drilling. I send him information about Great Britain's whimsical process of demarcation, transcripts of interviews from Vietnam vets, prepping him for the star treatment when he returns home with his shellshock and mysterious illnesses. He writes me letters of camaraderie, the spirit of freedom on the front lines, how you can feel it in the air, how you know freedom is worth fighting for because you can taste it. He writes how he happily pulls hundred and seven-hour shifts in a tank, sweating out the hours with dirty jokes and amphetamines. He writes me about what it was like to be part of history, to be part of a book, part of something real that everyone will remember for centuries, and when the war starts, he writes about how they had cruised along the trenches in behemoth vehicles just pouring the sand back in the trenches, doing away with whole regiments of Saddam's forces. They bury the sweaty fuckers alive without wasting any of their precious depleted uranium-tipped bullets. He writes of the fate of the ragheads who had tried to flee, only to taste the fury of M-16s, spinning and tearing through their flesh. Alex writes that their artillery does not gun people down, but literally rips people in half, and when people are ripped in half, it is not clean, like a blade, or a halved rump roast, but bodies burst and bubble, and it doesn't even look like meat. Alex writes about the adrenaline, the rush, the victory and a smell so odd and intense that it works its way in like nothing the sand can do. The smell gets in your nasal cavity and stays there, and even when you're back at camp, beating off in a lukewarm shower of non-potable water, you still can't get the smell out of your head.

"The good news," I tell the table—Jessica holds up her hand, but I can only hold out so long. I drain my chocolate shake and say, "According to multi-verse theory, there is an alternate universe where we don't even go to war, and Alex is free from proving his machismo. Of course, there is also a universe where Alex stays here and goes to junior college, and I get the hard-on for killing ragheads. *Seriously*," I say. "People thought Isaac Newton was a loon when he ran around talking about *gravity*. In time, in the future, the multi-verse will seem like common sense."

"Why do you talk about these things?" Jessica says. "I love you to pieces, and then you start talking about retarded things."

"This is legitimate quantum theory," I say.

"It's legitimate *dork* theory," Alex says.

Jessica says that you can't have a universe for every decision you make, that you can't just have a billion universes. She speaks with a milkshake mustache that makes her look both old and young at the same time. It also gives her a look that makes my stomach go cold. When Jessica was young, a robber had broken into her house and bashed her in the head with a fire extinguisher, shattering the top of her orbital bone. As a result, her left eye droops a little, a couple millimeters shy of grotesque, but instead gives her face that extra impressionistic flair that makes me crazy about her. I ask her why you can't have a billion universes.

"Because you can't."

"Why not?" Vanessa says. "If he believes it, it's true."

"That's not true either," I tell Vanessa. "Things don't become true just because you believe them."

"Yes, they do," she says.

"This is why," I tell them, drawing a diagram of a tiny dot, surrounded by two more dots, and explain to them that this is an atom. The vast majority is space, and these particles of matter actually breathe, they expand and contract. You don't have to stack one universe on top of the other, but you can layer them. You can live side by side these other worlds, and they can even be closer than that. They can be intertwined.

"Again," Vanessa says, "just nuke 'em."

Jessica tells Vanessa that we've changed subjects.

Vanessa says that when you die, you're worm food. "You people are driving me batshit. We need to get the hell out of here." She announces that she is going to the bathroom, and I'm surprised that it takes her this long. Every minute that passes, her body is absorbing molecule after molecule of nutrition, and it must be killing her. I want to tell Vanessa to wait, because I know what Jessica is going to say next—I can pull the words from her mouth like a sleeve full of scarves, and I do. Jessica says she is leaving. She gets up and walks out the door, and I know that I'm in one of those moments where you can reel time back and forth at will, where you can see the motivations and faultlines, actions and reactions. I can feel parts of me waking and slumbering and

I know that I can't go back to the Salad Station after ditching Vanessa, even though she walks out two minutes after us to the parking lot, untouched and unwatched. She doesn't even have the opportunity to let her ass get her out of the jam.

For Alex and me, the Dobermans are let loose. In the corner of my vision, I see Alex square up against a busboy—the asshole is completely ignorant of the fact that Alex is already fighting for his country—he gets arrested, and Uncle Sam is already one man down. The busboy has Alex by the collar of his shirt with his outstretched arm—not a bad move had he been gripping *me*, but Alex pulls him close by arching back then releases a flurry of fists, and that's all I need to see before cutting between the cars and bolting across the highway. I use a rare skill of being able to time speeding vehicles weaving in opposite directions, a skill the busboys lack, and they know it. Once across the six lanes, I stand safely with a raised middle finger. That's when I see Vanessa through the windows across the street, safely erasing any additional guilt by walking out of the double glass doors.

All of this is easy to see at the moment, in the present, sitting there, still at the restaurant, picking over the remains of our feast, and I know that I'll forgo the night's sleep before shipping Alex off to the war, and that he will be writing me letters about the desert, and that he'll write to me that his regiment had returned to the site of the war's beginning the following day to make certain that everyone had either been buried or slaughtered, and he had not expected to see what he had seen. I could practically read the letters sitting there in Denny's, his description of arms and legs sticking out of the sand—the scene had looked like some kind of horrific student art exhibition out in the middle of the desert—some of his fellow soldiers even stealing boots, and personal items, bullets and weapons, and in some cases teeth, and in every case gold teeth, but the scene had been surreal and spooky, but I did not expect to read his confessions or the fact that he remembered our conversation about the multi-verse, and that he had proof that I was wrong. He writes that it isn't a matter of a separate world where the enemy could have been him, but it was like returning to a site where you have physically removed your soul, then you hold your soul by the back of its invisible hair, then drag a knife across its neck from ear to ear, then bury it headfirst in the hundred forty-five degree sand. He writes that it was the first time he had ever felt light and heavy at the same time. I can read his letters from the Highway of Death here, too, sitting in Denny's, pushing our luck with a coconut cream pie, how he had not been there the day the jet planes strafed the strip of land from Kuwait to Baghdad, when the hundred thousand terrified Iraqi soldiers raced across the desert until they were reduced to teeth and carbon, but he shows up the next morning, with the task of walking through the mess of twisted metal and tanks and dismembered bodies frozen in horror, shooting anything that moved.

"Everybody knows it," he writes. "Everybody here knows it, but most people won't talk about it," and I know what he's talking about. He is referring to something I wrote to him in the beginning, that when you kill, you *kill*. You end the energy of a single life force, and whether you like it or know it, whether it is murder or not, justifiable or not, your own life force is affected, and your cells even know it, and your cells will remember that you have snuffed this force, and the killing will resonate for the rest of your life. Even Shakespeare knew it, which is why he did not allow his murderous characters to sleep. It's the inherent truth of a killer's insomnia.

One night after work, Jessica and I split a six-pack of Milwaukee's Best and a pack of 7-11 ephedrine. We rode our bikes across

Dunedin Causeway down to Honeymoon Island. By the time we reached the beach, the ephedrine had turned our hair follicles into ecstatic electrodes, lighting up like static glow when the wind blew, and the water even seemed to be in on the fun, as phosphorescence splashed along with us as we swam out to Caladesi across the shark waters in mysterious dayglo green. It was one of those warm Florida winter evenings, when the water runs cold and nothing is feeding on the food chain. The sharks are down there, but they are letting us have our time. We held on to each other at times, our legs kicking, our knees and ankles knocking together, sometimes locking together in simulated bliss. We returned home, back to the rat trap on Douglas, both of us itching something fierce from sand and saltwater residues. We soothed our stings with the burn of Seabreeze, and that's when they made the announcement on the radio about the beginning of Desert Storm. That night we slept under a single sheet on the same bed, and in the morning, she was on the telephone.

By May, the correspondence between Alex and me had ended. Once, later in the summer, I saw Alex's mother at Publix. We were both buying Cheerios. And then one afternoon near the end of summer, I saw Alex hitching up U.S. 19. He was all the way up in Tarpon Springs, near Klosterman on the opposite side of the highway. As I passed, I could see that his teeth had gotten longer as he shielded the sun from his eyes with his hands and looked for possible rides. He was wearing a plain white T-shirt and blue jeans. I could tell it was him in a second, and my heart juggled around in my chest for a couple hard strong palpitations, and I jerked a U-turn halfway to Alderman. It was a hot, Florida August. My car would provide no relief, as my '66 Falcon with the windows down was nothing but a moving convection oven with the A.C. a solid decade in decay. I wondered what Alex was doing this far north of Dunedin. Jessica had moved back with her parents, and Alex's parents were in Clearwater, but I imagined that there were a probably a hundred reasons why he could be there or anywhere. I tried to catch up to him, but I was on the inside lane, and a Cadillac full of geriatrics blocked my attempts to change lanes and reach him. I tried to pass them, but they edged closer up on me. Then for some reason, I slowed down and got even with them. When they looked at me, I made a gun sign with my hand and pretended the shoot them all, one by one. The action seemed absurd, and foolish, and perhaps dangerous, but it had also taken me out of the moment. By the time I gotten into the far right lane, I had again passed Klosterman Road again, and looking back in the rear-view mirror, I could see Alex still there on the side of the road, shielding the sun from his eyes, scouting down a lift.

All the Way from Junaluska

The year before, all of the rooms and the foyer at the Methodist Center had looked out upon the glass surface of Lake Junaluska, reflecting Blue Ridge mountaintops with such clarity that you could take a picture of the lake, then flip the photograph around, and find it impossible to tell which way was up or down. In fact, one of the high school students had snapped one of these photographs on the last day of the trip when it had snowed, and the image had appeared almost as a monochromatic etching, with stark white against stark blacks. Everything in the photograph appeared black and white, except for a small red trailer situated on the north shore. It was the only reference point of direction. The student ordered a poster-sized print of the picture, framed it and hung it in the Sepulveda Baptist Church youth group study room.

That was the year before, when the Sepulveda Baptist Church first sent their youth group to the retreat at Lake Junaluska, where they had fellowshipped with dozens of other youth groups around the country. The high-schoolers had taken canoes out on the water in mid-winter right up to the edge of the dam, where the water skimmed a millimeter from the top. Floating bits of twigs, dead leaves, bits of bark and gunk swirled up from the bottom. The water parted halfway down the back of the dam, and some of the kids had scaled the forty feet to the top. That was the year before, though, before the lake had been drained.

The following year, after engineers had emptied the lake, the inside face of the dam resembled the Coolidge Dam, but on a smaller scale, and was nevertheless a monolithic wall of concrete. The lake now ran in a meandering stream down the middle of the bed of the lake, which transformed into a spectacular spider's web of cracked and frozen mud. A black line ran along the top third of the dam. When the youth group arrived at the Center, they had to wait in the lobby for keys to their rooms. TJ, a tenth-grader, had asked Palmer, their youth pastor, what the black line was, and Palmer said it was a pipe. He said it was a pipe that goes from one side to the other, and if anybody walked from one side to the next, he would buy the entire camp pizzas. Every youth group in attendance. Free pizza for all. Palmer thought about this while having a cup of coffee on the third day, as he sat in the lobby waiting for the cafeteria to open for lunch. He thought about this dare as he counted five teenagers scooting their feet across the pipe that he guessed was a foot, maybe a foot and a half in diameter. The little bastards. He wondered if he had actually promised pizza, or if his tone had been obviously facetious. Either way, he was not going to buy pizzas for the entire camp. He thought for a second that he could possibly swing little personal pan pizzas, which might only set him back a few hundred dollars, but that would probably be worse that stiffing them altogether. All his credibility would be shot. When TJ had asked him what that pipe was, he should have said: "It's a pipe, TJ." *What's it for?* "I don't know. Probably transferring sewage water from one area to another area." Or simply: "Sewage," he could have said. "It's for sewage, TJ." But he had not simplified it. He had tried to crank up the fun, add a layer of excitement and lay out a dare.

"Sewage, TJ," he said out loud, sitting in the foyer, watching the teenagers inch their way across. "It's for damn sewage," he said again, then looked around to see if anyone had heard him.

Of course, failure and cowardice were always on the table. The teenagers could always turn back, and Palmer focused his energy on this possibility and even cast up a little prayer, asking Dear Lord to please help them not make it across. He then changed his prayer and asked that the kids make it across the dam, and that he find five hundred dollars somewhere in this backassward town. Then he asked the Lord to simply provide, and thanked Him for sending His Son to die on the cross for our sins, and that in the whole scheme of things, the pizzas were not that big of a deal and that if it helped somebody get to know His Son, then all the better, but five hundred dollars ...

When Palmer looked up again he counted four teenagers. Had there been four or five? Had there been three? Had one returned? One had gone back. Hudson had gone back. Hudson was gone. He had been there. Palmer had recognized Hudson, Willingham and John Kittmer, along with two others. One down four to go. They had been clipping along. Inching along, but clipping as far as inching goes. But now there were four, because one had gone back. He glanced at the top of the dam and along the edge of the former shoreline. There had been five, but now the four had dropped to their crotches and appeared to be hugging the pipe, reaching down with their hands in the motion of a beckoning. Palmer sat up and took a breath. One of them dropped, purposefully. He could tell by the way the teenager caught himself spiderlike and had to perform a couple of quick Navy Seal-type maneuvers before steadying himself and creeping downwards.

Palmer refilled his Styrofoam cup of coffee in the cafeteria before he walked down to the dam. He knew also that if he did not make a sandwich to go, then he might be hung up all afternoon without food. The canteen, however, had reached a low point: yesterday's white bread, with yesterday's deli meat, with yesterday's lettuce and what looked like last week's tomatoes. Even so, he made a double-decker and ate half of it standing in the coffee line. He swirled in cream and two sugars, then pressed on a white plastic lid and headed back to the window.

The cold hit him as he stepped out of the double glass doors. He buttoned his jacket as he walked. The pipe, as he could see on the walk down the driveway and onto the access road, was clear of teenagers, who had begun to gather on the road passing over the dam. Some of the kids leaned over the rails were waving their arms.

Palmer revised a lecture in his mind about responsibility and common sense. About how he could instruct them on the rules of safety but that at some point they would need to be proactive. They were scheduled to head up to Chimney Rock on the last day of the retreat, and if they couldn't handle a single dam without risking life and limb, then how could they handle gazing at God's creation from a three-hundred-foot rock jutting into the sky? How could they stop by Sugar Mountain on the drive home for a day of skiing, with ski lifts, snow machines, the Diamond Run, and all kinds of ways to do yourself in? He wanted to slap them in the head and tell the little fuckers to *think*, but once John Kittmer spotted him he picked up his pace and, when he was within earshot, he tossed the coffee into the dried winter brush on the side of the road.

* * *

When the paramedics arrived, they said they needed a diver, or hooks. TJ was still on the backside of the dam waiting for anything to pop through, and the paramedics said what they needed first and foremost was to contact the caretaker of the lake and get him to plug the dam. They needed to shut the dam so they could stop the flow and get the godforsaken water to stop frothing, and then they could go in from the backside, and they would have a hell of an easier time with the hooks in the pool. Of course the hooks wouldn't be much good with all the froth.

John Kittmer suggested they just tie a bunch of blankets together and dive into the froth and try to see what they could find, and the paramedics said to get the goddamned kids away from the dam, and that nobody was going near the froth. Palmer reminded John Kittmer that it was twenty-eight degrees out, and the paramedics reminded Palmer that if he didn't get the goddamn kids away from the scene, they would call him in. What they needed was to get hold of the caretaker and plug the dam. Call the caretaker and get the hooks. Call the caretaker and get the hooks and get the goddamn kids away from there. Somebody said something about a chopper, and another person said they didn't need any goddamned chopper.

The sun, which had been shining brightly just moments before, had just slipped over the mountains and threw them suddenly into dusk. The mountain shadows cast darkness upon them even though the sky still shone bright blue, and any heat trapped between the mountains was evaporating quickly.

According to John Kittmer, if Hudson had fallen to the left, he probably could have caught himself against the incline, just a five-foot drop—he could have at least have had the chance to spreadeagle and scrape himself to a halt. But he hadn't. He had fallen to the right, and by the time he made contact with the concrete, he had already dropped ten feet and gained such momentum that he bounced and tumbled, which would not have been as bad had he fallen to the side of the stream, but the concave shape of the dam had bounced toward the center, and the white water had swallowed him in a single *whoosh*.

One of the paramedics asked John Kittmer what they were doing up on the pipe, and John Kittmer said they were trying to win pizzas. Palmer interrupted John Kittmer and said that teenagers think they're invincible. For some reason, nobody thinks they can die at age seventeen.

When darkness came, they set up the portable flood lamps that made the scene look like the set of a Hollywood movie. The other youth groups in the auditorium held a special prayer meeting. Palmer's group had cleared the scene but had brought plenty of blankets and set them out on the mud-cracked surface of the lake's dried bottom. The fire chief had tried to contact the caretaker, but he had gone to Richmond for a wedding. There was a message on his answering machine. His cell phone kept going straight to voicemail. They had contacted the wedding party, but the caretaker had yet to arrive. Once he arrived, they could tell him to turn around, but that was once he got there. Palmer asked if they didn't have anybody else who could plug the dam, and they said there were plenty of people who could plug a dam, but they didn't have the keys, and it wasn't just a matter of plugging the dam, but a matter of machinery … and the closest town was Asheville. Not Durham. Not Charlotte. *Asheville.*

* * *

The teenagers were gathered close, and Palmer thought about leading a prayer, then decided he would wait a while. One of the girls had come back from the hotel with candles, but a man in a fireman's uniform spoke into a megaphone and instructed them to immediately extinguish the candles. TJ asked why they couldn't use candles, and Palmer found himself beginning to tell TJ that they couldn't use candles because the fireman was a fascist, but he caught himself and said they couldn't use candles because candles use fire, and fire spreads when it comes in contact with flammable materials, and their blankets and clothes were flammable. *That* was why. Then he caught himself and reiterated the fireman's message, telling him that the fireman said they couldn't use candles, so they can't use candles. Just sit tight and wait. That's all they could do.

Then TJ asked him if what John Kittmer was saying might be true, that there might be a chamber down there inside the dam and that Hudson could be inside the chamber. Was that a possibility? TJ asked and Palmer told him to just sit tight. They needed to get in touch with the caretaker, he told TJ. He's on the way to Richmond, and they've got to get him back.

* * *

On the way back to his room, Palmer asked the concierge if he could have access to the kitchen in order to make some kind of sandwich, and the concierge said the cafeteria was closed. Palmer told the concierge that he was the leader of the party with the accident, and the concierge told him he did not want to get fired.

In his room, Palmer opened a ginger ale and made the phone calls. He did not want to leave until there was some kind of closure, or a more definite answer. On the way back to the lake, he stopped by the cafeteria to double-check, and he discovered that the concierge was right, the cafeteria was closed. The lights were out, but the doors were open, as were the doors to the kitchen. When he turned on the switch, the fluorescent lights hung in the halfway zone, as if they could not decide whether to turn on or stay off, creating a feeling of suspension. He found some hard-crusted sourdough, struggled to slice off two pieces with a standard kitchen knife, and prepared a ham sandwich with a slice of meat and a quick zip of mustard, just to take the edge off his hunger. He also dipped into the egg salad, which had a slight funk to it. He passed this off as the funk of sourdough, but by then it was too late, and he slugged this noxious concoction down with a half-pint of chocolate milk, which left a tang of cow aftertaste. *Cripes*, Palmer thought. *How the hell does somebody lock down a little freshness in this joint? The hell with the countryside*, he thought. *Pristine air, my ass. Stale bread and death traps everywhere you looked.*

The students assembled around Palmer, who led prayers asking for Hudson's safety. He reminded the teenagers that we are insignificant, and that we need to stay in fellowship. He prayed for common sense to be bestowed upon the students and asked for them to understand that their actions had consequences, and that we are not alone—nobody is alone—and that we need to think before we act. He thought for a moment about his dare, the great pizza challenge, and he swallowed the last bit of prayer and asked if anybody had anything to offer.

They did. Willingham, one of the kids who had ventured out on to the pipe, said that we need to remember who Hudson is and who God is. He spoke to the teenagers and said that if it sounded like he had not been crying it was because he had not been crying. He stressed to his friends that the lucky one was Hudson. If what John Kittmer was saying was true, that there was a chamber, then Hudson would have a heck of a story to tell. If Hudson is not in the chamber, then he is with already with the Lord. He is in Heaven, and how lucky is that? That's where we all want to be. Either way, it was God's will. Wasn't it reason to rejoice? Wasn't everything a reason to rejoice? Willingham said that, actually, he was jealous.

Palmer wanted to tell him to dive in, then: *Hop on in, kiddo. Nobody's stopping you.*

Palmer could see the concierge making his way down from the driveway, so Palmer walked his direction and flagged him down. Pastor Fink had called, and a group of parents were on their way up. The instructions were to stay put until these parents arrived, and then take everybody else back home in the van. Palmer still had the smell of milk rot lingering in his nasal passages, and knew that if he could make it four hours with that egg salad kept down in his belly, then he could pass it all the way through. Until then, he would have to fend off psychosomatic nausea. The concierge asked if they needed anything, and Palmer said that everyone was fine, that they were set, but once the concierge made his way halfway up the driveway, Palmer realized that only he had eaten anything, and that perhaps he should have asked around to see if anyone else were hungry.

John Kittmer stepped forward and said he had something he wanted to announce. Hudson should be lucky to have so many people care about him, he said, and added that he had good news: Hudson was alive. John Kittmer spoke of how disappointed he was that so many people had assumed that Hudson had drowned.

"Listen," he began, and he told them all about a field trip he had taken with the engineering club. They had gone to the Skyway Bridge to take a tour of the massive support columns, and he discovered that inside these columns were stairwells that went way down below the water's surface. He was in no doubt that there was a chamber inside the dam. If there only existed a single pipe, then the pipe would have clogged up long ago, and the water pressure would have blown everything out the backside. Dams don't work that way. He said that the water enters a chamber, like a pool, accessible to people like scientists who can go inside to take samples and what not. There were probably even emergency lights. Even if not, Hudson would be able to float to the surface and climb out. He told the kids that Hudson was down there. They needed to get him out, and they would; he could feel it.

From the shadows, a young girl screamed that everybody was a bunch of assholes. It was Hudson's girlfriend, Bailey, and she screamed that Palmer was an asshole, that John Kittmer was an asshole, and that everybody was just a bunch of assholes.

Bailey was not a member of the Sepulveda Bible Church, and Palmer had spoken with Hudson about her on multiple occasions. Hudson had told him that she was agnostic, that she wanted to believe in God but she couldn't. He thought that in the end she would see, and Palmer had been supportive. OK, he had said, bring her along. But if you bring her along, then emerge unscathed if it doesn't work out. If it doesn't work out, then emerge without VD, without AIDS and without a baby, or without getting an abortion. Palmer had gone so far as to take Hudson out for coffee, to explain in the clearest terms he could find the draw and danger of carnal desires. Bailey was certainly equipped with the goods to tempt—the perfect ratio of an over-developed bosom with hips that were still ten or fifteen years from matching the circumference. He told Hudson that you could even smell her daddy complex a mile away, and though girls like that needed love, they also spelled trouble.

"Emerge as one, or emerge unscathed," he had said.

Bailey screamed at Palmer as he finished his prayer and demanded to know why he wasn't in the water. He should be in there looking for Hudson. She got up, and came over to him, kicking and punching out at him, administering blows to his forehead and wherever else he was vulnerable. He reached out to protect himself but was conscious of avoiding the type of physical contact that could be considered offensive, or illegal. He first secured her left elbow, then maneuvered his grip to her wrists. She then swung her arms wide and came at him with her mouth, opened and ready to bite, to which he responded by dropping to his knees and forcing her upper body to the ground and motioning to John Kittmer and Willingham to take her back to her room. By the time they reached the access road, he could see her walking on her own.

The floodlights reflecting from the surface of the dam were so powerful that Palmer had to shade his eyes. From where he stood at the top of the dam, the teenagers below looked like a pack of jackals waiting in the shadows. Palmer could see that the meandering stream was not so small, and that it picked up speed as it reached the dam. Anyone who fell from this position would almost certainly bounce off the angle and curvature of the dam, into the pool of froth.

The Fire Chief approached Palmer and asked how he was holding up.

Palmer said he was fine. "What are the odds?" he asked.

"The odds of what?" the Chief said.

"That he's down there," the youth pastor said.

"Where else could he be?"

"Is there an air bubble?"

The Fire Chief said there were about a hundred billion air bubbles. That's what the froth was. But there was not a bubble big enough for anybody to stick their head in and breathe.

"No air pocket?"

The Fire Chief asked Palmer what the hell he was talking about.

Palmer said he had heard about natural phenomena where air gets trapped.

The Fire Chief said there was no natural phenomenon down there.

"Well, where is he?" Palmer said. "Where's Hudson?"

The Fire Chief said it was difficult to determine. The boy could be under it all, churning, or he could be snagged on rock or rebar, or he could be stuck in the pipe at the bottom of the dam.

Palmer told the Fire Chief that one of the students had a little engineering background, and thought there might be a chamber inside the dam.

"What kind of chamber?"

"A chamber that might function like a weigh station for the water."

"A weigh station?"

"Or, like a pool. So scientists can test the water if they need to."

"Why wouldn't they just test the water outside the dam?"

"I don't know," Palmer said.

"I don't either," the Chief said. "The water doesn't need any weigh station. The water needs to go from one side to the other."

"Then why did they open the pipe?"

The Fire Chief said they pull the plug every decade or so to clear the silt. They empty the lake, then 'doze out the silt. It takes months but, if they don't 'doze out the silt, then it backs up, and then they don't have a lake, they just have silt.

Palmer said that if Hudson were stuck in the pipe, why wasn't the water backing up?

"It is backing up," the Fire Chief said. "It's backed up about five feet already and already risen a foot."

"Then how could he still be churning or stuck on rebar?"

"He probably isn't, but I don't want to say anything definite until the caretaker gets here and we can either shut the dam or divert the water."

"So he might be plugging the dam."

"We've been monitoring the situation. Those kids'll have to clear out. If he's plugging the dam, then the water's going to stop churning at some point, and we can get him out. If that's where he is." The Fire Chief nodded toward the kids. "You don't want them here if they pull out the body. You're going to need to clear them out as soon as possible. Anything can happen at this point. All of you need to back up, get back up the hill and clear out."

Those parents can just turn around once they get here, Palmer thought. *Pick up their kids, then turn around and drive straight back to Florida.*

Hudson's parents were the only ones who needed to be there. Palmer couldn't figure out why the other parents wanted to come up.

He gave the teenagers thirty minutes to pack, and thought they could make it to Atlanta by the time the sun came up. By noon, they would be home in Palm Shades. He could take care of the responsibilities required of him, which would probably allow him to sleep sometime the following day. He chose John Kittmer and Willingham to corral the kids and get them back up the hill. Thirty minutes to departure. He told them the trip to Chimney Rock was off. The day at Sugar Mountain was off. He heard a few groans. He told the teenagers that he would have Mary-Anne back at the church make all the phone calls and reserve their tickets for next year or get some kind of refund, but pack up. The bus pulls out by eleven. That could get them out of North Carolina by midnight.

Palmer knocked on Bailey's open door, went inside and sat on the television stand, leaving the room door propped open with a suitcase. "It's been a bad day," he said.

Bailey, who had been sitting on her bed, stood up dressed only in a T-shirt and her underwear. She reached down to pull on a pair of snow pants.

"There. You've seen me. Happy now?"

"Bailey," he said, but she walked past him into the bathroom and closed the door. Bottles and tubes clinked and jostled from bag to porcelain surfaces to another bag, then silence, then more moving of bottles and tubes, then a faucet and nylon bristles against teeth.

"Today is a very bad day, Bailey," Palmer said through the door. "I'm not going to lie."

"Please," she said.

Palmer paused for a moment. "If you'd like to pray we can pray."

The sounds from the bathroom stopped for nearly a full minute. "Do you want to pray?" he heard her say.

"Yes," said Palmer.

"Then pray."

He paused before asking if they would be praying together.

"Do you want to pray together?"

"If that's what you want," Palmer said. "But, yes, I think we should pray together." He waited for a response, and then the door opened and she said to come in and sit down.

"We pray here," she said and closed the door behind her. "We can pray here, and whatever happens happens."

"Bailey," Palmer said.

"You can start anytime you want to."

Palmer bowed his head and thanked the Lord for bringing Bailey into the fold, for her company and fellowship, and asked the Lord to guide her through her dark hours and to realize that everything happens for a reason, even though we don't understand the reasons at the time, and as a result of what seems like a tragedy, what is a tragedy, a lot of good might come from it. There are people here this week who have never known You, and who know that the time to get to know You is now, and there might be angels rejoicing at this very moment, and if Bailey doesn't know You, then allow her to see that You have given Your Son to die for her sins that she may have everlasting life. "Amen."

Palmer paused, then looked up and saw that Bailey had indeed bowed her head as well, and she began. She asked the Lord to forgive Hudson, to forgive Palmer and to forgive all of them. She asked the Lord to allow all of these people to stop being so obsessed with getting to Heaven, and start learning how to be normal people. "Amen."

Palmer looked up at Bailey. "You need to rest," he said.

"What you need to do is wake up," she said. "That's what you need to do, and that's what everybody needs to do."

"Actually, Bailey, you have no right."

"I have every right," she said. "What are you doing? What are they doing? We're up here on a retreat, and what is everybody doing? Everyone is supposed to be here dedicating their lives to Christ. Fine. If that's what you want to do, or what Hudson wants to do, then that's fine. But *do* it. We're up here meeting people from all over the country, everybody is talking about acting as agents of God's will, and what are we doing? We're goofing around. We're fucking off. Where does it say that in order to dedicate your life to Christ that you have to walk on a pipe across a fucking dam? In order to eat free pizza. What are we doing? We're having sex in the pump house and getting stoned on cough syrup. They're passing Seven-Up bottles filled with vodka around the back of the bus."

Palmer said she could interpret events the way she wanted, and what she needed to do first was feel the feelings that she needed to feel, nobody had any right to tell her how to feel. And when she got back to Florida she could come by the church and talk to him anytime she wanted, or she could talk to Pastor Fink, or Assistant Pastor Hamilton if she wanted, or she could even talk to their secretary if she would rather speak to a woman.

"I've made the phone calls, however, and there are some parents on the way here. They'll be here soon, and we should be home by about lunchtime tomorrow." It was not a lie, he knew, but he was simply floating the truth out there, so he told her: "I've been in touch with the parents, and someone'll be giving you a ride back to Florida. You can ride with Hudson's parents maybe?" he waited for a response.

"We prayed," she said. "You can go."

Somehow, Palmer got hooked onto the Blue Ridge Parkway instead of I-40, which was the last thing he needed. After the second harrowing Blue Ridge downhill burst, Palmer decided to call Pastor Fink and tell him that he had been through the mill, that he was not in the proper mind to talk to anybody, that he was traumatized, and that he needed some space, but why would he need to tell him that if he had been traumatized?

The fact was that he hadn't yet called Pastor Fink. He hadn't yet made the phone calls. He would call Pastor Fink when they needed gas. When he got in touch with Pastor Fink, he would tell him what happened. He would say that he had seen the teenagers on the pipe, and that he had high-tailed it down to the lake but that Hudson had dropped before he could stop them. He would tell him that five kids and a fellow youth group leader from another church had to hold him back from jumping in himself. He changed his mind, and decided he would tell Pastor Fink three had held him back. For the moment, he wanted to know why the roads had been built on the goddamned inclines that seemed designed for maximum terror, and each time they reached the top and had to go back down again, the teenagers hoo-ed and squealed, even in their advanced stages of grief, as if he needed no concentration at all, the winter-stripped trees streaming by on the sides of the road, him tapping the brakes when the steering wheel shook too hard and dragging the engine at the bottom gear. If the teenagers wanted to grieve, then *grieve*, he wanted to tell them, but shut up for two minutes. Shut up for two goddamned minutes.

The road leveled off, and the sign said eighteen miles to I-28, and Palmer turned off the radio. He thought about the trip they had taken to North Carolina the summer before. How they had hiked seven miles up the mountain, drunk water from mountain streams, camped overnight and then driven back to Florida the following morning. The rains had come on hard that year, but most of the kids had run around anyway, which was fine, but on the way back they had been on a dirt road winding through the mountains, when half of the road had been washed out on one side. The van could have tumbled, but inertia had carried them just far enough into the brush. The van should have tumbled, the more he thought about it, and sometimes this thought came back to him. He couldn't do anything, the road wet and slick and soft without any kind of warning, but still the kids subsequently razzed him the entire drive back, all the way to the Sepulveda Bible Church parking lot. Some of the parents had spoken to him about it several days and weeks later, and asked why he hadn't reported the incident.

Why? Because there was no pleasing some people. That's why.

By the time they hit the South Carolina state line, he twice slowed down with a real mind to stop, walk to the back of the bus and just start swatting every kid in sight. The little pricks. They weren't even asleep. They were singing. They had been singing ever since they had finally gone on to I-28. They sang "This Little Light of Mine," they sang "Raise Him Up" and "Amazing Grace." They sang "As the Sun Doth Daily Rise," and they sang "O Render Thanks to God Above."

With a quarter tank of gas left, Palmer finally pulled over. What he wanted to do was to swat TJ first with an open hand, and then give John Kittmer a broken nose to praise over. He would have trouble with Willingham. If Willingham fought back, it would be worth it. He would lose going up against Willingham, but at least he would go down swinging. As he sat there contemplating, with his head on the wheel, he felt the sensation of a hand on his shoulder.

Palmer had been touched before. Once, walking through the woods, before seminary, he had been touched. A hand on his shoulder, but when he had turned around, he had seen nothing. Nobody. A supernatural presence, maybe, but he had been touched. But this time, it was John Kittmer, smiling with the light of the gas station illuminating his face, and the dark of the bus behind him.

"Palmer," John Kittmer said. "We have good news. We all could feel it a few miles back there. We could feel it all the way from Asheville. Hudson's alive. The Lord told us. He was in the chamber all along. He's alive. A bunch of us have already talked about driving back up once we get to Florida. We could feel it clear as day. He's alive."

Dogs

Dogs appeared on the opposite side of the lake. Dogs, not deer, though there was some speculation. Dr. Finch said that they were probably deer, but Dr. Craig said that he wasn't so sure. They looked like dogs. The cows wading in the black water across the lake noticed as well, and with the arrival of the dogs, the collective mood of the herd appeared to shift.

"Those are just a bunch of deer," Marlon, said, Dr. Finch's thirteen year-old son.

"Those are dogs," Marlon's friend, Digger, said. "I think they're dogs."

"Are they dogs?" Dr. Craig said.

"Oh, my God," Mrs. Finch said. "That's a pack of dogs."

"Goddamn it," Dr. Finch said.

Above the water, martins darted in random patterns, gorging on mosquitoes, and clouds took on a purple hue as the sun appeared to have, just moments prior, decided to set. The dogs seemed to understand that if they wanted action, the time was now, and they bolted in unison into the water. The cows, once lumbering, clumsy beasts, chose flight over fight and transformed into near-graceful machines, clearing out of the lake, hugging the lip of the water around the far side near the fence.

"Goddamned dogs," Dr. Finch said, as Marlon and Digger stood up, watching the cows, nearly a half-mile away, over a hundred and fifty of them, make their way around the lake in a surreal dreamlike wave, turning the far corner.

Digger wondered if Marlon felt the same sense of rapture,

both startled and fascinated by the terrifying speed of the cows and the ease with which the dogs wove in and around the frantic herd.

"They're going to come right at us," Digger said.

"They'll stop," Marlon said, which struck Digger as an absurd comment. Why would they stop? They might barrel into the lake, they might get cornered and start stomping dogs, but the event simply dissipating without reaching some crisis point was clearly out of the question.

When the cows reached the fence that bordered State Road 48, they had no choice but to turn left and gun it. Dr. Finch, his son and his son's friend, his wife, and Dr. Craig, stood on the porch watching as the cows, several hundred yards away, heading directly towards them and gaining speed.

"They're going to kill us," Mrs. Finch said.

"Jesus Christ," Dr. Finch said.

As Dr. Craig shouted at the dogs, Dr. Finch continued cursing, Mrs. Finch suddenly cleared the plates and headed inside, and the four of them stood, hearing the stampede grow from a sonic rug, like a mass of African drummers in the distance, to a rolling thunder, creating concentric circles on the surface Dr. Craig's cup of coffee. The cows formed a front line, twenty or thirty yards wide, with the dogs barely visible, dodging hooves and legs. Then, with fluid precision, the cows parted and ran past the trailer and into a barbed-wire fence topped with electric wire, which had been designed to merely discourage the cows from crossing into the neighbor's property, but by no means engineered to stop a literal stampede. Dr. Craig leaned over the railing trying to scream, but instead uttered a high pitched, barely audible shriek, the band of blonde hair lightening against his reddening face and bald scalp. The beasts jumped, tripped and poured across the fence. Some cows tangled their hooves, jerked and tugged and broke free, and others fell on the wire, then twisted and contorted wildly in an awkward orgy, and a few danced through the pandemonium in a moving display of idiotic athleticism. Dr. Craig grabbed his pack of cigarettes, pulled one out and lit it without looking and said, "Jesus Christ, Lee. You gotta fix that. Goddamn it, Lee. You gotta fix this. This is not good. This is not good at all."

Dr. Finch worked under Dr. Craig, who spearheaded a team of researchers developing designer milk at the University of Alabama, Birmingham. The process involved injecting cows with human antibodies to create a type of super-milk that theoretically killed off everything from cancer cells to the common cold. One of Dr. Finch's responsibilities included driving out to the farm in Ashville twice a month to administer injections and collect cases of blood samples. At the lab in Birmingham, the researchers fed the milk to baboons and tested their recoverability. From time to time, Dr. Craig showed up on Dr. Finch's designated weekends for inspections, which generally included fly fishing, pheasant hunting and drinking beer. Some of the researchers at the lab had even pooled money together to stock the lake with bass. Dr. Craig had a habit of leaning on the porch railing, huffing down cigarettes and Heinekens and exclaiming, "Lee, this is great. This is really great, here. Goddamn. Fantastic. Just great."

Digger agreed with Dr. Craig's sentiment. Whenever the Finches spent the weekend at the trailer, Marlon's parents allowed him to invite a friend along. Up in Ashville, the boys were allowed to roam free on the property. They fished the spillway. They camped on the opposite side of the lake. They tried to catch snapping turtles using hunks of beefsteak on gigantic hooks tied to milk jugs for bobbers. They melted Coke bottles in campfires, hunted and swam in the lake. They conducted crude experiments on the fish pulled from the spillway, clipping the fins from catfish, stuffing baby bream with firecrackers. The boys flipped turtles on their backs to bake in the sun and pitted crawdads and frogs in mini-epic death matches. It thrilled Digger each time he was invited.

The property that the cows spilled into belonged to the Fountain family, or the Frankies, as they had come to be known in town. When Digger returned from weekends in Ashville he could entertain his family for entire meals with stories about Little Frankie Fountain, son of Big Frankie Fountain. He would spin Frankie yarns to his neighborhood baseball crew, who pressed him for details and demanded the retelling of stories, searching for cracks and loopholes. And Digger never had to embellish— in fact, Frankie antics demanded understatement and the downplaying of events in order to even keep his subjects properly engaged. Most of the stories began with a loose variation of, "Keep in mind, Little Frankie, eleven years old, traveled with a gun in his boot, one on his hip, and a rifle on the dashboard of his jeep."

Little Frankie operated on the philosophy of doing things to see what would happen. When he was nine, to *see what would happen*, Little Frankie had pulled the lever to the cherry picker while his father was repairing power lines on the far end of the property, dumping his father forty feet to the ground—ending the days where Big Frankie's right knee knew the pleasures of full extension. Once, while camping out with Marlon and Digger, he had reached into the coals to pull out a nearly molten Coke bottle, burning his hand to the meat. For this same reason, Frankie had put sugar in his father's gas tank, enclosed an M-60 in his fist, and once, to see what would happen, he marked off fifty yards exactly, to see if birdshot really traveled that distance, handing Marlon his .20 gauge, only to learn that bird shot travels just *past* fifty yards. The last time Digger and Marlon had gone swimming with little Frankie, hundreds of off-white scars on Little Frankie's chest, camouflaged by a hundred thousand pimples, proved it. Frankie's presence loomed all over Ashville, and when he came over, there was no tip-toeing into Frankieville; chances were, he would hop out of his still-moving jeep screaming that his 'nads were fried from pissing on that electric fence. (Digger had been in the Frankies' house once, and immediately he became a believer. Digger had never seen a home so equipped with firearms—in every room. Rifles leaned against the living room wall, shotguns leaned in the corner of the den, shotgun on the mantle, Colt .45 next to the coffee maker, a Luger on the TV, silver-plated this, nickel-plated that, scopes on the love seat, a slingshot in the bathroom, and even a crossbow next to the dining-room table. In the basement, Big Frankie had rigged a machine loaded with pounds of gunpowder, which he used to make his own hollow-tip .45 bullets. When Little Frankie showed them the machine, he had taken out his lighter and said, "Watch this!" and pretended to hit the flint. For days, Marlon had a stoic, vacant look about him and would suddenly say, "You just don't do that. You just don't play games like that." It was the single occasion Digger had witnessed Frankie practice restraint, and he made note of it.) When the cows bulldozed into the Frankie's property, Digger half-expected the entire Frankie family waiting, barrels poking out of slit curtains, infrared goggles, itchy fingers, and everyone from Big Frankie to the family dog strapped down with bandoliers and homemade hand grenades.

* * *

From the trailer porch, Marlon and Digger could see the two researchers fly-fishing across the lake. The two watched in amazement the frequency with which the two men caught fish.

They cast, cast again, cast again, cast, catch, release, but even in dusk and from that distance, it was clear to the boys that the Dr. Finch and Dr. Craig weren't speaking. One could sense their clenched jaws from five hundred yards. The cows, in their panic and desperation to regroup, had destroyed or knocked down portions of the fence for a quarter-mile. Waist-deep in the water, the researchers waded fifty yards out and cast towards the far shore. Digger asked Marlon why didn't they just stand on the shore and cast out, and Marlon asked him how the hell he was supposed to know.

Digger said that each time his dad or Dr. Craig released one of the fish he could feel a small part of himself die.

"You want to hear the stupidest part? You want to know why they let the fish go? To impress each other. They have to act like even the biggest fish they get is nothing compared to what they're used to catching. Sure. And I'd bet that if either of them caught one of those fish by themselves, they'd cream in their pants." Marlon explained that it was the same way in his dad's lab. Every time his father, or one of the other scientists made any sort of progress, breakthrough, or completed any kind of report, they had to pretend it was no big deal, like it was all a matter of course. "Plus, you know, half the time my dad comes home from work, he's bitching about Dr. Craig, and how the guy's on the rag *all* the time. He's like, 'Goddamn it, Lee, one of the baboons got scabies! How the hell does a baboon get scabies?' And of course, my *dad* got the grant for this milk experiment, and this guy didn't do dick, but he gets twice the dough, even though it's my *dad* that's gotta come out here and look after everything. You know what my dad is? He's a caretaker. Get that. He studies his entire life, works his ass off to get this goddamn grant, and what do they make him? A caretaker."

"How *does* a baboon catch scabies?"

"It doesn't matter. The point is that chances are dickwasher out there's gonna get the patents if these experiments turn out to be successful, since my dad's on his staff. Like Edison. Then Dr. Craig comes around here, and he's like, 'God, Lee, this is great.' Where's Dr. Craig when we gotta run a goddamn electric wire over three miles of fence? Where's Dr. Craig when we fish all Frankie's goddamn mannequin parts out of the lake? Yeah, of *course*, it's great."

Digger paused, removed one of Dr. Craig's cigarettes. "You think your mom will see if I smoke this?"

"Nah. Probably not. I don't know. *Probably*."

"Good smoke," he said, lighting up.

"Gimme some of that," Marlon said, dragging, then blowing smoke through his mouth and nose at the same time.

"Maybe that experimental milk gave the baboons scabies," Digger said.

"The milk didn't give anybody scabies."

"How do you know?"

"Because milk doesn't give people scabies."

"Maybe *that* milk does."

"You had that milk for breakfast. I have it everyday. Jesus Christ." Marlon took the cigarette and gave it another drag. "Look at them out there. They might as well be arm wrestling, or see who can lift the biggest rock."

* * *

Morning fog hovered just above the lake, and Digger noted a single martin flying just over the surface of the water. Dr. Finch poured a cup of coffee while Mrs. Finch cooked bacon, eggs, orange juice and biscuits. Dr. Finch said that he had talked to Big Frankie, and word was that a bunch of rednecks drive thirty or forty miles from their portion of God's-ass-armpit and drop off their dogs in another part of God's-ass-armpit when they want to get rid of their dogs. "And now these fuckers have sort of banded together. They've made a pack. Like goddamn wolves."

Mrs. Finch warned her husband about his language, and he explained to her that in no uncertain terms were those dogs anything *but* fuckers, and he would give them fifty dollars for every dog they killed. That was the deal. Fifty per head.

"Regular dogs?" Marlon said.

"Just dogs," Dr. Finch said.

"House dogs." Mrs. Finch said. "They looked like house dogs."

"Not godforsaken poodles, but dogs. I was kind of preoccupied when I saw them yesterday, with a herd of cows threatening to bury us. I couldn't really make out any definite breed."

Marlon asked his dad whether or not Dr. Craig thought the dogs were great or not.

Dr. Finch asked Marlon if he wanted to crawl up and yank that gigantic hair out of Dr. Craig's ass. The two boys hushed, and Mrs. Finch said that it would take her about two seconds to pack the boys in the car and drive them home if he continued to use that kind of language.

* * *

Just as Dr. Finch asked aloud where the hell Frankie was, the jeep pulled up, and Frankie unlatched the gate, then eased the jeep up to the porch. Frankie hopped out on one foot, explaining that not five minutes ago, his big toe was about as stuck as stuck can be in the biggest rat trap he'd ever seen. "They should call those things cat traps," he said, then continued an exaggerated limp. Dr. Finch glared at Marlon and Digger until their hysterics settled down to silent shrieks.

"We need to obtain some control over this property," Dr.

Finch said. "It doesn't matter how successful your research is if you can't run your shop." Dr. Finch explained to Little Frankie that shooting the cows up with tranquilizers and crap wasn't the best idea if they wanted pure tests results. He did not need jumpy cows, he needed calm cows. They needed usable test results. He explained to Frankie that he was a *scientist.* "We're talking hormones, we're talking antibodies, and when animals, whether it's you or me or those fucking cows, the endocrine system has a habit of getting thrown out of whack when dosed with high levels of tranquilizers." Dr. Finch sipped his coffee, then said, "And the exact same thing happens when their blood is constantly pulsing with adrenaline. Why is it so difficult to establish a goddamned baseline?" He explained to Little Frankie that he did not need to deal with any more departmental bullshit than necessary, and that once you earned a reputation of having wild dogs ruining all your experiments, then assignments and fellowships and professorships tend to get redirected, and that investors in the private sector begin to give you funny looks—a point that seemed to be completely missed on the young boys. Dr. Finch asked Little Frankie if he had ever tried to draw blood from a moving cow, and the two boys looked at each other, knowing that he had asked precisely the type of question that, in an attempt to fix one problem, might create several unfixable problems.

Dr. Finch reiterated the deal. Fifty dollars per dog. He told Frankie that if anybody in his family wanted to try their luck during the week, he would pay them, too. Frankie thanked Dr. Finch and reminded him that his dad wanted to meet sometime and discuss the fence.

By eleven in the morning, the foreheads of Marlon and Digger had dotted the windshield of Frankie's jeep with over seventeen small spider webs. They once narrowly missed the steel extension of a rusted-out combine that jutted just above the windshield after driving through the back wall of an abandoned barn. They went rut riding. They went trail making. Frankie showed them his stash of porn magazines, which required them to actually climb down inside a well, fingertips clinging to crevices and feet feeling for footholds in the dark. He showed the two boys how to pull apple trees by connecting a chain to the base of the trunk. He let Marlon have a go. He let Digger have a go, screaming in his high-pitched southern squeal to "Keep it in low gear! Keep it in low gear!" Then he said they should quit, since they were his dad's prized apple trees, sending images through Digger's mind of a middle-aged man, doing his best, limp and all, to sprint after them, then dropping to his belly with a .44 rifle, taking careful aim, then dropping the three of them one by one. The boys made napalm by mixing siphoned gas and Styrofoam. They placed .22 caliber bullets on the railroad tracks to see what would happen. They drove up a gravel driveway onto private property, an old semi-dilapidated house situated close to a pond on the side yard carpeted with lily pads and green foam. A wall of kudzu separating the back yard from the woods had completely engulfed a car, swelling it to the side of a shed. An area with a radius of about seven feet had been worn down to packed earth, except for an iron post with a rope tied to a boxer mutt that seemed to be paying the three boys careful attention, legs slightly apart, as if it were not quite sure if the interlopers had shown up to play or attack.

Frankie jammed on the gas, burning a donut on the front lawn. "Get the hell out of here," Marlon said.

Frankie braked, pointed to the sign in front of the pond. "What's that sign say?"

"No swimming," Digger said.

"Why? You think it's deep?" Frankie asked.

"They probably just don't want a bunch of yahoos coming out here and jumping around in their pond," Marlon said. "Like you two."

Frankie explained that if he drove fast enough with two side wheels in the water and the other two on land, he could make a spray like Hawaii Five-O, and before Marlon could protest, Frankie gunned the accelerator and hit the pond at such an angle that the two driver-side wheels immediately sank and flipped the jeep into the water. Digger mistook his submerged moments for death itself. In fact, the moment when he had freed himself had occurred during a complete blackout. How had he known to climb out? How had he climbed out? A lost, weightless feeling, warm and confused until light and sound rushed upon him. Marlon and Frankie were already arguing on the side of the pond, soaked. When Digger climbed to the edge, he looked at the pond. It only took moments for the surface to regain its calm. The pond, now plus one jeep, appeared clueless as to the violence that had been afflicted up on it one minute before.

"That is a very old jeep," Frankie said.

"You almost killed us," Marlon said.

"Nobody got killed."

"You could have killed us," Marlon said, and Frankie disappeared into the water and returned with the BB gun. "The other guns are gone," he said. "Big Frankie's going to kill me."

"You call your dad Big Frankie?" Digger said.

"Yeah, he's Big Frankie," he said, then dove back into the water and returned with his .22. "Thank God," he said. While he inspected the gun, he informed Marlon and Digger that standing water ponds in rural Alabama are among the most contaminated in the country, that if the green water tasted like pesticides and fertilizer, it's because that's what it was.

"Years of accumulated fertilizer and pesticides," Marlon said, speculating aloud that amoebas probably sit in there and stew, mutating into the kind of super-microbes that get in your ear and cause brain damage.

"That's right," Little Frankie said.

Near the house, the dog barked, legs still apart, but tensed. The boys looked at the dog. The dog barked again and continued barking.

The next afternoon, when Digger would walk down the hill to scare up a game of five-on-five neighborhood baseball, he would take special care to develop his story. He would show his friends the lacerations on his forehead and a black and blue nebula on his shoulder, special delivery care of the dashboard, then stumble upon a technique in storytelling that one usually discovers later in life that offers instant believability—the backpedal. "Oh, no … no, no, it didn't really happen like that—oh jeez, no, not like that at all"—as if overstatement had ever been in the recipe of Little Frankie tales. "Let's divvy up teams," Digger would say, but they would be hooked. They were engaged and determined to see a resolution.

"He's going to shoot the dog," Digger said to Marlon, while Frankie alternated between taking aim and gazing down the barrel of the gun.

"Probably," Marlon said. "He's Frankie."

"It's not one of the *dog* dogs."

"Probably not. But look at that rope. "You know what I'd say if I was tied up like that for life?" Marlon asked. "I'd say take me out. Put a bullet in my head. Make it quick. If you have any compassion, cut me loose or kill me."

"Let's cut it loose," Digger said.

"Then it'll join up with the rest of the pack and become one of the wild dogs. We'll have done the exact opposite as what we were supposed to do."

"Those dogs would probably gang up on it and tear it into oblivion," Digger said.

"Or let it join," Marlon said. "Strength in numbers. They'll initiate it, but eventually, it will become part of the pack. Dogs are social animals. It's in their nature."

"Mm," Digger said, looking at Little Frankie who repeatedly took aim at the dog, then pulled the gun away.

"Either way," Marlon said. "We have to shoot it now. If we set it free, we're counterproductive. If we don't set it free, we have to act out of compassion. That dog is suffering. Dogs need to roam. Besides, God gave us dominion over animals."

Frankie declared that he was prepared to take the first shot.

"I thought God cared about everything down to the sparrows," Digger said.

"Oh, *now* God cares about the sparrows, now that you're not tossing live catfish into the coals. Of course He cares about the sparrows, but He still gave us dominion over them."

Little Frankie put the rifle down. He lifted the .22 up to his shoulder again, then took it back down. Digger and Marlon watched the boy muse. They saw that Little Frankie was in his true workshop, and then Little Frankie said, "Why don't we just cut off a foot? We'll bring a foot back."

"Nobody's cutting off its foot," Digger said. "Nobody's cutting off any feet."

"Why not?" Frankie said.

"'*Cause*," Digger said.

"Hold on," Marlon said. "We could let it live that way. Dogs live all the time with three feet. Maybe they would feel sorry for it. Give it a longer rope. It's a hell of a lot better than killing it."

"Who's going to cut it off?" Digger said.

"Frankie," Marlon said.

"I'll cut it off," Frankie volunteered.

"With what?

"Pocket knife," Frankie said, holding up a six-inch jackknife.

"Christ, where do you keep these things?" Marlon said.

"Boot."

"I thought you carried a pistol in your boot?" Marlon said.

"Other boot."

"Jesus," Marlon said, while Digger giggled.

"What happened to the pistol in your boot?" Digger asked, and Frankie pointed to the pond. "How come the knife didn't fall out?" Digger asked.

"Good luck, I guess," Frankie said.

Frankie explained that it would be easy. He could grab the dog's leg, pull it away from the dog, and the rope would keep its head back far enough away to keep from biting him. He scraped the knife against his forearm and shaved a small fluff of soft white hair and declared that it would take one flip of his wrist and that would be that. The dog would barely feel anything. He'd snip it off between the joints.

"He's right," Marlon said. "Plus, you're buying its freedom. We let it go, we gotta shoot it. We keep it here, we gotta shoot it. It's win-win for everybody. Do it quick. He won't feel it."

"Like hell he won't," Digger said. "That dog's gonna go into shock."

"Dogs don't go into shock," Marlon said.

"Why not?"

"Have you ever heard of a dog going into shock?"

"No."

"See?" Marlon said. "Dogs fight. Dogs kill. Dogs get killed. Just cut off the fucking foot, Frankie."

"I'll bet my fifty he feels it," Digger said. "I'll bet Frankie's fifty, too."

"It's fifty each?" Frankie said.

"I think so. It's fifty each, right?" Digger said to Marlon.

"It's fifty total," Marlon said.

"I think it's fifty each," Digger said.

"It's fifty each," Frankie said.

"I'm not paying anybody fifty dollars each," Marlon said.

"You're not paying anybody anything," Digger said.

"This is not about fifty bucks each," Marlon said. "If you two dimwits paid any goddamn attention, you'd know that it's my dad's job we're talking about. Dr. Craig is already so far up his ass that he can barely get anything done. You think this place is so great, Digger? Cut off the goddamn foot. You think this place is so fantastic? You're just like Dr. Craig. Stop hemming and hawing. Fifty bucks is an aspirin my dad is taking to get that asshole off his case for two seconds."

Digger and Frankie looked at each other.

"You like to come out here and raise hell, but how do you think it happens? Who makes it happen? Who makes this possible for you, Digger? Cut off the goddamned foot."

Frankie crouched down ninja style behind the dog and swooped in with deceptive speed for an overweight country boy in soggy jeans. But not swift enough, as the dog retracted his foot and tore into the back of Little Frankie's hand.

"Jesus God," Marlon said.

"That dog is fucking dangerous," Digger said.

Frankie held his hand tight between the crotch of his pants screaming inaudibly, until tears welled in his eyes. He kept his sobbing at a minimum, though, walked down to the pond, rinsed his hand, filled his wound with untold amounts of paramecia and returned.

"You're going to need a doctor," Digger said.

"And an antibiotic," Marlon said. "You're gonna need a shot."

"You're going to need so much antibiotic there won't be any room for your blood," Digger said.

"He's right," Marlon said.

"*You're* gonna go into shock," Digger said.

"Enough with the shock already," Marlon said.

Frankie swooped in a second time and the dog bit his forearm. The young boy jumped backwards, tried to hit the dog in the head with the butt of the rifle, but the dog grabbed the gun with its teeth and tugged it from Frankie's hands.

"Get the BB gun," Marlon said. "I'll stun it, and you grab the .22."

"I'll stun it, *you* grab the .22," Digger said.

Digger pumped the gun ten times and shot the dog in the hindquarters.

"Shoot it in the goddamned eyeball or something," Marlon said. "Don't shoot it in the ass."

"I'm stunning it."

"Stun it in the *eyeball*. Don't fuck around."

Frankie pounced in, kicked the gun and the dog bit the back of Frankie's thigh.

"Stay away from the fucking dog, Frankie," Digger said, just as Frankie scooped up the gun, and in one motion set his feet, took aim and shot the dog in the shoulder with the .22. The shot punched the dog backwards as if it had been hit with a bowling ball, and the dog scratched at the ground to regain its balance, yipping, then producing a low, vibrating, guttural howl.

"Oh, my God," Marlon said. "You two are like the Three Stooges. If you're going to do it, do it. If you're going to kill it, then kill it."

Frankie splashed a bullet in the meat of the dog's hindquarters, and then pierced a back paw. "That thing bit me," Frankie said. "It's gonna pay a while before I kill it. I'm gonna get a stick."

"You tried to cut off its foot," Digger said. "Of course it's going to bite you."

The dog coiled back as far away from the three boys as possible, its tail curled up tight between its legs. The dog peed orange urine on its own downy white belly. The skin above its teeth jerked up and down as if a drunken three year-old were pulling them from invisible strings.

"Just shoot the thing in the head and get this over with," Marlon said.

"I'm going to shoot it straight through the heart," Frankie said.

"Shoot it in the eyeball," Marlon said, just as Frankie fired a bullet just below the collar.

Blood had beaded into little balls of dirt, along with small puddles and streaks of black that the dry earth refused to absorb. The dog backed up as far as the rope would let it.

The dog bled more than Digger realized a dog could bleed— maybe a quart, maybe a gallon. Where the dog stored its energy to coil and thrash about was beyond his understanding. What was clear now was that the dog had to die. All gray areas of mercy killings for a dog with border frustration had been eliminated. The dog's suffering now fell under the category of *significant*. Little Frankie had run out of .22 shells after all of his superfluous firing, and they were forced to rely solely on the BB gun and a broomstick Frankie had found to which the jackknife had been affixed. With nearly an entire box of BBs, they took turns pumping and firing. They pumped and fired. They aimed at the dog's eyes, ears, mouth and nose. They hit their targets and they missed. They aimed indiscriminately, and the dog seemed determined to endure the entire supply. Marlon's watch had drowned in the pond, and it was impossible to tell the exact time. However, by the position of the sun, the three boys agreed that it was only just past lunchtime, just passed noon, and the entire afternoon stretched out before them.

Acknowledgments

"*No Rabia*" originally appeared as "*No Rabio*" in *The Gettysburg Review.*

"Home Fries" first appeared in *The Madison Review* and was previously published by Blue Cubicle Press

Versions of "Does Anything Beautiful Emerge?" were published by The Head and the Hand Press and *YARN.*

Versions of "All Eighty-Eight Keys" were published by *upstreet* and The Head and the Hand Press.

"Stripping Roses" was originally published by *The Baltimore Review.*

"Hypothermia" was originally published by *CutBank.*

"All the Way from Junaluska" was originally published by The Chicago Center for Literature and Photography.

About the Author

Tim Fitts lives in Philadelphia with his wife and two children. Fitts teaches in the Liberal Arts Department of the Curtis Institute of Music and serves on the editorial staff of *The Painted Bride Quarterly*.

Fitts was born in Dallas, Texas, and grew up in the South, spending his childhood in Shades Mountain, Alabama, then moving to Clearwater, Florida until finishing college. During Fitts' college years, he spent years playing music and spent two years working extensively in the Sycom studios at the University of South Florida. Fitts' photography work can be seen at the Thomas Deans Gallery, in Atlanta.

His stories have appeared in numerous national literary journals, and his story "No Rabio" was selected as a Special Mention in the 2013 Pushcart Prize. *Hypothermia* is his first published collection of short stories, and his novel *The Soju Club* was published as a Korean translation.